PENGUIN  (

T0163183

# BLEEDING SUN

Rogelio R. Sicat left his hometown San Isidro, Nueva Ecija, in the 1950s to work on a degree in journalism at the University of Santo Tomas. After serving as a campus writer and literary editor of *The Varsitarian*, Sicat went on to become one of the greatest pioneers of Philippine fiction by deliberately choosing Filipino as the language of his prose, and by veering away from the concerns and conventions of the Western modernist writers. Sicat's work, which rejuvenated Philippine literature's tradition of social consciousness, first appeared in the Tagalog literary magazine *Liwayway*. He gained recognition in the Palanca Awards in 1962, and in 1965, came out in an anthology, *Mga Agos sa Disyerto*, alongside like-minded young writers. Sicat wrote on through the decades, establishing his position in literary history as fictionist, playwright, and professor, eventually accepting deanship in the University of the Philippines Diliman. *Impeng Negro* and *Tata Selo*, both of which have been interpreted into films, are only two of Sicat's acclaimed stories. His other works include *Pagsalunga: Piniling Kuwento at Sanaysayand* and the play *Moses, Moses*. Sicat died in 1997, but was honoured a final time through a posthumous National Book Award the following year for his translation of William J. Pomeroy's work into the title *Ang Gubat: Isang Personal na Rekord ng Pakikilabang Gerilya ng mga Huk sa Pilipinas*. He was married to Ellen Sicat, a former certified public accountant, and together they have five children.

Ma. Aurora L. Sicat is the second of Rogelio's five children. She earned her Bachelor of Arts in Filipino degree at the College of Arts and Letters in the University of the Philippines Diliman. She has worked for GMA Worldwide, Inc., as a freelance translator where she translated their Tagalog television programs and movie shows to English. She also ventured into freelance writing and copywriting but has now retired.

# Dugo Sa Bukang-Liwayway
# Bleeding Sun

## The Tale of a Farmer's Crushed Dreams and Hopes

Rogelio Sicat

*Translated and Edited by*
Ma. Aurora L. Sicat

PENGUIN BOOKS

An imprint of Penguin Random House

PENGUIN CLASSICS

USA | Canada | UK | Ireland | Australia
New Zealand | India | South Africa | China | Southeast Asia

Penguin Classics is part of the Penguin Random House group of companies
whose addresses can be found at global.penguinrandomhouse.com

Published by Penguin Random House SEA Pte Ltd
9, Changi South Street 3, Level 08-01,
Singapore 486361

First published in Penguin Classics by Penguin Random House SEA 2024

ISBN 9789815144505

Typeset in Garamond by MAP Systems, Bengaluru, India

www.penguin.sg

# Contents

Introduction
*vii*

Part I
Tano and Simon–Father and Son
*1*

Part II
Escape
*45*

Part III
Return
*87*

# Introduction

## Virgilio S. Almario

*Rogelio Sicat's close friend, Retired professor of Philippine
literature at UP Diliman, distinguished book author and poet,
National Artist for Philippine Literature*

Every written work is imbued with the personal touch of the
author; a window into what's going on in his world, which
shows through the crevices of his work. Not to bring Freud
and Jung and other famous psychologists and scholars into
this, who would attempt to diagnose a writer's subconscious
and examine how his past experiences moulded him into the
person he is today. We can say that even if the author was
wearing a thick mask, his fingerprint-like impression left on
paper can help a scholar or critic identify his reasons or the
inspiration behind his work.

In the case of Rogelio R. Sicat's *Bleeding Sun*, he forged
his manuscript with blood, sweat, and tears and has ultimately
left his footprints in the world forever. His hometown,

San Isidro, Nueva Ecija, is analogous to San Roque in the novel. Deductions can be made through his characters, that affirm the 'authenticity' of his voice in his writings. Echoes from his personal life can also be heard in the lives of his characters.

It is possible that the novel may even be read as Sicat's own biography. It could very well feel like interpreting a dream, as Freud did: the life and the novel of the author seem to be related to each other. For example, Tano could be Sicat's father (Estanislao B. Sicat). However, his father was educated and served as the Secretary of the municipality. Tano, on the other hand, is but a poor unlettered farmer, with no land to his name. But the love that Estanislao had for his son; his great efforts to send his son to school, were in the same vein as Tano's upbringing of Simon.

Let's talk more about Sicat.

He was born on 26 June 1940 in Alua, a village in San Isidro, Nueva Ecija. He was sixth of Estanislao and Crisanta Rodriguez's eight children. Unlike Tano, who is one of the main characters in the novel, a peasant who lived from hand to mouth, the Rodriguez family was middle-class. On Crisanta's side, they were heirs of a large farmland, but when the time came for the land to bear fruit, when the family was in dire need of finances, they were forced to sell it. This is not unlike Paterno Borja's genealogy in the novel.

Sicat grew up in a house with a spacious yard. From the backyard, one could see the Pampanga River close by. Sicat's father was adept at fishing and they would often go to the river to enjoy fishing together. This memory of their extraordinary father–son relationship, is reflected in Tano and Simon's unusual closeness while Simon was growing up. The wisdom that Sicat had acquired from his father was not unlike what Simon learned from his. Sicat also appears to reminisce about glorious childhood memories in his novel, especially in the descriptions of how Tano and Simon wrestled with one another sometimes.

Perhaps Sicat's father did not wrestle with him. Nonetheless, the memory in the novel stands as a symbol of his fondest childhood memories with his father, until he went to a public school in his hometown.

Sicat had started taking interest and showing an expertise in literature while he was still in high school. Leopoldo C. Gonzales, an English teacher from the same town, encouraged Sicat to write. Sicat then started sending his short stories to *Liwayway*, and articles to *Philippine Free Press*. *Liwayway* was a Tagalog literary magazine, which enjoyed a long history, and many writers aspired to have their articles published in it, since it was quite the institution in the country. Sicat gained more and more self-confidence every time one of his works got published. This was likewise felt by Tano in the novel upon noticing Simon's diligence in studying.

He became the editor-in-chief of their high school newspaper at General de Jesus Academy. Afterwards, he won *Liwayway*'s writing competition for students. Sicat grew increasingly motivated to continue writing. He went on to write plays, in which he worked as both a performer and a director. He was a prolific writer also because he loved reading. He would read almost any kind of literature—Edgar Allan Poe, Shakespeare, Alphonse Daudet, John Keats,

Percy B. Shelley, William Wordsworth, Lord Byron, Guy de Maupassant, etc.

He continued to pursue his passion for writing by taking up journalism at UST in 1959 where he also served as the literary editor of the student's paper *Varsitarian*. Afterwards, he applied as an apprentice at *Liwayway*, where he was promoted to work as a proofreader. He considered himself lucky for having landed a job that would help him hone his talent as a writer. This promotion brought him closer to other young writers, who would later help him write many articles about contemporary issues. He continued to inspire Filipinos and his students to appreciate Philippine literature while teaching at the College of Arts and Letters (CAL) in UP Diliman. He was not only remembered as a faculty, but a good adviser and Dean of CAL as well. After his death in 1997, his legacy continued through annual creative writing workshops for budding writers in Filipino.

## San Isidro/San Roque

Sicat's novel is not entirely a biography, either. San Roque, where *Bleeding Sun* is set, is not a replica of San Isidro, Sicat's own hometown. A work is not made any more 'real' by a writer's personal experiences being reflected in it. A writer could be influenced by a host of other factors in his environment that inspire him to write. Subconsciously, he might compare and contrast these experiences with his own through language, distortion, and exaggeration of situations and characters, through fast and slow pacing, and several other literary tactics and devices. He used the formula of conflicts and elements that would otherwise entertain, thrill, or surprise the reader.

Sicat's works fall under the genre of realism. We understand realism to be contradictory to what is false; writing that is based on facts, reflects what is going on in the world, which explains why sociologists and critics read literary works as if they were reading the newspaper. They even claim that a realist work is a reflection of the writer's milieu—an important ingredient for the genre.

Let us take a look at San Roque, a fictitious town, and examine the ways in which it is similar and dissimilar to San Isidro.

Like San Roque, San Isidro is also an agrarian town. Rice fields cover more than four thousand hectares of its area. Some fields are planted with vegetables, corn, watermelon, sweet potatoes, and fruits. Albeit it was formerly included in the province of Pampanga, most of its townsfolk are Tagalog. Allegedly, this migration was brought about by Tagalog farmers and their families.

Like San Roque, San Isidro also witnessed the cruelty of World War II. Moreover, the town was a hotspot of agrarian movements against the unjust administration overseeing the rice fields.

While it is true that *Bleeding Sun* is a novel about agrarian reform and a social commentary, it is also the story of Simon, a farmer's son, who was born in a poor province, grew up with no mother, was orphaned after his father died before he could graduate from high school, fell in love with an elite woman, ran away from home, and returned bearing a silent desire for vengeance against his parents' oppressors. It is likewise a story about two of his childhood friends, both of whom also come from poor families: Ador, who perseveres to become a teacher to help his town, and Duardo, who seeks solace among the insurgents. Tano, Elena, and Ador support the cast. The novel would not be authentic or real if the characters had a happy ending, and if it solved the problem of agrarian reform.

It is true that Sicat referred to historical events while writing the novel, but his desire to write an epic—a Filipino epic—shines through, with only passing mentions of the Spanish, Japanese, and American Occupation in the Philippines, to offer the reader a glimpse—and no more—of what transpired during WWI and WWII and the period that followed. One must take this primary intention of the author into account while reading the novel. Furthermore, he offers a view of the rural life in San Roque using folktales and sayings he gathered, and likewise uses natural elements to propel the narrative.

San Roque appears to be a dark and gloomy place. One can see the farmers' sincere desire to own the land they till, and yet their language has neither the melodrama nor the brute force that is traditionally associated with reform movements. We can see, in fact, the reverence Tano has for the land he tills, treating it as a precious thing he almost worships, and unhesitatingly devotes his entire life to. The rest of the farmers, too, nurture the hope that their condition would improve.

# Part I

Tano and Simon–Father and Son

1922

The year was 1922. World War I (28 July 1914–11 November 1918) had ended. The Philippines had earlier been in its Spanish colonial period for 333 years between 1565 and 1898. Prior to the conclusion of WWI, the Treaty of Paris (December 1898) was signed, ending the Spanish–American War, with the Spaniards selling off the Philippines for $20 million to America.

The American government then became the new colonizers of the Philippines. Later, in 1936, Manuel L. Quezon was inaugurated as the President of the Commonwealth of the Philippines, the second president after Emilio Aguinaldo, whom he defeated in the 1935 elections.

That day, the sun's rays were scorching hot. The clouds seemed like they were overinflated with condensed air and were about to implode. No wind was blowing—there was not even a sign of a breeze; everything was still. The muddy and rocky paths were dry and cracked.

*It's going to rain*, Tano thought as he stood by the fields trying to predict the weather. Based on a farmers' weather forecasting system, when it got unusually hot, such that one felt like they were inside an oven, a heavy downpour was to be expected.

Tano was like any ordinary farmer whose skin had tanned from labouring for long hours under the sun. In both his hands were sheaves of seedlings. His long-sleeved shirt showed wear and tear, and his trousers, ending just below the knees, were soiled with dry mud.

His legs were shaking. He had patiently been planting the seedlings the whole day. Like other farmers, he was moving swiftly because they did not own the land and hence were not too eager to cultivate the best crops. Nonetheless, growing rice was their livelihood, their bread and butter, their only means of survival. Their only choice was either to work to survive, or starve to death.

Tano still had a lot of seedlings left and wanted nothing to go to waste. He would not spare any spaces—that would ensure a bountiful harvest.

*It's going to rain!* Tano gleefully mused. He got a bird's-eye view of the vast and layered fields. Up above, blankets of dark clouds were gathering fast. *My, it's going to rain sooner than I thought.* In a little while, the winds blew the clouds over to the mountain. It would rain soon, no doubt about it, and his almost-wilted plants would be quenched by its cold water.

After the seedlings were planted, Tano stretched his arms and took a last look at the land he had tilled. As he stood upright, he gave a sigh of relief. There were no more vacant lots—he had cultivated the whole plot. It was time to go home. There was excitement in his heart. He could not wait to see Melang, his wife.

He went to a nearby lake and threw his native rice planter's hat on its bank. With both hands, he scrubbed and cleaned his hair and the sleeves of his shirt. He took a dip in the lake and used his big, calloused palms to scoop up water to scrub his face, arms, thighs, and legs clean. He began to walk out, the mud in between his toes leaving footprints on his path. He walked through the cultivated fields until he reached the national highway. While walking, he looked again at the lot he had tilled and wondered—even though it was too early to say definitely—who would be the farmer with the most bountiful harvest, and who would come home empty-handed. There was a silent voice inside him that hoped he would be among the peasants who got to bring home lots of harvest. He only had a few debts to pay off to his comrades and it was finally harvest season. But Melang was due to give birth soon, and to offer a fitting welcome to the new family member, he needed to produce more crops.

It was already midnight when Tano arrived at their hut, which stood in a small yard. At the rear, beside a huge tree, was the makeshift pen of a carabao. Behind the pen was a river, which extended itself into the ocean.

'It's going to rain, Tano!' his wife cheerfully greeted him as he entered through the door. Tano was much older than Melang. Her long hair was tied neatly behind her head so house chores could be carried out more conveniently. Her youth had not faded completely but there were already traces of wrinkles in her face. She was a woman of short stature. The hem of her red dress was tattered. She walked slowly, carrying the weight of the baby in her womb with some difficulty.

'You can bet on it, Melang,' Tano said. 'What's that for?' he asked when he noticed his wife holding cocoa leaves.

Melang smiled. 'While you were in the field, I felt contractions. Ka Tindeng said this would do the trick.'

Soon enough, the rain started falling hard, just as Tano had predicted. And at last, he and Melang were going to have a baby. Melang had been pregnant twice before—once she had had a miscarriage, and the other time a still birth. She was a bit like Tano's farm—his crops would sprout, but in the absence of rain, they would wilt. Farmers welcome the rain after a long, hot summer day—just like Tano was ready to welcome his baby!

Tano's wife used to work with him in the fields, but as her condition became increasingly delicate, he began to fear that overtaxing at the farm could have serious repercussions for her and their child. That was when Tano decided it was best his wife stayed home while he became the sole breadwinner. Even so, Melang never stayed idle at home. Their hut was never in disarray; she would always mop the bamboo floor clean of dirt and dust, and make sure the kitchen sink was cleared after every meal. Whenever Tano came home from the farm, he would catch Melang sewing clothes for the baby, sitting beside the window. Around midnight, when they would lie down to rest, Melang would take his hand, unable to contain her anticipation, and let him feel her bump when she felt the baby moving.

'I hope it's a boy,' Tano would say.

The first time Melang had got pregnant, she had wished for a baby girl. 'I hope it's a girl, Tano, I want a daughter,' she had said. However, after two miscarriages, she conceded to Tano's request.

It was still raining at night after the light showers in the beginning had turned into a storm. Tano watched the rain under the bright lantern. As the downpour became heavier, he closed the shutters of the window. When he turned towards the kitchen, he saw Melang's plump figure carrying a basin.

'What's that for, Melang?'

'I will collect water from our leaking roof.'

'There's a storm outside. The rain is good for my plants,' Tano remarked.

'Thank God!' Melang exclaimed. 'Tonight, the rain will finally quench our crops. The hope of good harvest is timed perfectly with the arrival of our child. Have you thought of a name?'

'We will call him Simon. I will cradle him in my arms the whole day. I will not let the barren Maria carry him because her sweet words might spoil the little boy. And when I feel tired, I will lay the baby in the hammock you made. Rest assured that I will take good care of him.'

It continued to rain throughout the next day's afternoon. Strong winds followed. The windows of their hut, made with palm leaves, rattled. The wind threatened to sweep the roof off the hut and permeate the cogon grass.

The cocoa leaves were boiling over hot charcoal. The leftover leaves from the lot Melang had boiled earlier had cooled down, so she was boiling another lot. Tano was wide awake, staring at the wall, waiting for the moment. Anxious, he stared at the burning coals. He had been longing for the rain before, but why did it have to come now when Melang was about to give birth? She was having contractions again and they had become more frequent. At her side was the basin with the water she had collected. She suddenly faltered and Tano rushed to lay her down on a mat.

'I think you better call Ka Tindeng, Tano,' Melang said. 'It hurts. Do it now. Call her.'

The most anticipated moment had come. Tano could not move from his wife's side for a while, but upon seeing the restless Melang unable to settle down and once again scream in pain, he panicked. He couldn't think straight and was fumbling as he tied the strings of his raincoat around his neck. He then grabbed his wide-rimmed hat and glowing lantern. He needed the lantern to guide his way through the dark and rainy night. The wind was blowing relentlessly through the heavy downpour, lightning and thunder booming as he walked along the road.

Tano had to wrestle against the rains. He could hardly keep his wide-rimmed hat on, his lantern swinging wildly in the strong winds. He felt like he was trying to go through an impenetrable wall. His shirt was soaking wet— his raincoat could hardly protect him.

Finally, he arrived at the midwife's house. Upon learning the news, they both rushed along the bumpy road back.

'How long has she been having contractions?' the midwife asked. Ka Tindeng was a middle-aged woman, almost the same age as Tano. She was carrying a bag with sterilized scissors, cotton balls, gauze, and thread to cut and tie the umbilical cord. Three months ago, she had herself given birth to a baby boy.

She held her wide-rimmed hat in place with her right hand while trying to balance her feet on the ground.

'Let's hurry, Ka Tindeng,' Tano urged her on.

Upon reaching the hut, Ka Tindeng pulled Melang's dress up and pinned it on her side. She asked Tano to bring a basin of boiled water and a face towel.

Melang was groaning in pain, fists clenched, unable to pacify herself. 'Ka Tindeng,' she held on to the midwife's arm as she gasped beside her. 'Oh, oh, Ka Tindeng.'

Ka Tindeng dropped her tools on her lap. 'Calm down. Leave everything to us.'

'Ka Tindeng . . .'

The rain had not stopped, but the midwife's forehead was dripping with sweat.

'How is she, Ka Tindeng?' asked Tano.

She could not answer him. Tano once again stared at the fire, in anticipation and fear of what might happen. He added more wood to the stove. *I hope it's a boy, Melang. Dear Lord, please help Melang. I pray for her safe delivery. I really hope everything's going to be okay.*

Tano looked at the midwife, then at his wife. He could hear Melang calling his name. She was groaning in pain but Tano remembered that Melang typically had a difficult labour. This was exactly what had happened the last time, when she had had a still birth. Melang's arms were trembling. Her head tossed around on the pillow and she barely had any strength left to push the baby out.

'How is she, Ka Tindeng?'

The midwife could only stare at Melang. Ka Tindeng brushed away the wisps of hair falling over her eyes, still looking at Melang, and called out to Tano.

'I think you better call the doctor, Tano.'

'Doctor?'

'Run to town. Fetch the doctor.'

Tano tried to stay calm but he was panicking. He once again donned his raincoat and grabbed the lantern. He tried to look for his wide-rimmed hat but could not remember where he had left it.

He stepped outside and braved the storm once again. The rain was lashing against his face. The glowing lantern could hardly lighten his path. The town was far away.

He returned with the doctor, who was carrying an umbrella.

'We need to take her to the hospital,' the doctor calmly decided after examining Melang. 'She's losing too much blood.'

Tano stared at the doctor incredulously. 'Hospital? Why do we need to take Melang to the hospital, doctor? Doctor, please help Melang.'

'I cannot help her here, Tano.'

'How can we take her to the hospital now? It's too far.'

The doctor could only nod in agreement.

'If we use the horse carriage, she might not be able to make it, doctor.'

'You can borrow Borja's car. I will accompany you to the hospital.'

Tano hesitated to go near his wife. He then grabbed his lantern that he had left at the door. He stepped outside and then back inside again, trying to remain calm. He had forgotten to take his raincoat. Behind him, lightning flashing through the darkness could be seen. Aside from Melang, Tano was now also worried about Señor Borja. Would the rich man let the poor man borrow his car? Why would he entertain a peasant like Tano?

*He will let me borrow his car,* Tano thought. *He cannot refuse.* But what if he was turned down? Only Señor Borja owned a car in the whole town of San Roque. What if he refused?

*He will let me borrow his car,* Tano reaffirmed to himself. *Please let me borrow your car, Señor Borja. Señor Borja, for Melang's sake.*

Tano arrived at Señor Borja's mansion in town. The windows of the huge house were closed and so was their gate.

'Señor Borja!' he screamed.

The dogs were alarmed and started to bark. Tano looked up at the huge house, looking out for any human figures who might hear him, but he did not see anyone. No one turned on the lights. He banged on the gate. The rowdy dogs barked more loudly. After a few minutes, Tano saw someone turning on the lights. Someone descended the stairs. From the heavy steps he heard, he was certain it was Señor Borja.

'Good evening, Señor,' Tano greeted resoundingly. 'Good evening.'

Señor Borja rubbed his eyes, trying to see him; he could not figure out who was calling his name and why at such an unholy hour.

'Who is it?!' Señor Borja asked at the top of his voice. He did not move from the stairs.

'It's Tano, Señor.'

'What do you need?'

'Señor Borja, may I borrow your car? My wife is about to give birth. I need to take her to the hospital.'

Señor Borja yelled at the barking dogs to quiet down. He placed his stout palms at the back of his ears. 'What did you say?'

'It's Tano, Señor Borja. May I borrow your car? My wife will die if I don't take her to the hospital right now.'

Señor Borja finally got the message. 'You mean in the middle of a storm? You have no idea how difficult it is to drive in this kind of weather.'

'My wife, Señor Borja, she will die.' Tano softly pleaded. 'I beg you.'

Señor Borja shook his head. 'I'm telling you, it's impossible to drive in this kind of weather. Just call the doctor.' He poised to turn away.

'Señor Borja,' Tano banged on the steel gate. 'Señor Borja!'

Borja climbed back up the stairs. He turned off the lights. Darkness spread and the glow from Tano's lantern turned pale. The dogs began barking once again.

The rain had started to slow down, but it was still dark when he returned to the village. The whole place was quiet. The only thing he could hear was the streaming water in the drains. From time to time, there were streaks of lightning in the sky.

*What now?* For a while, he felt confused. One by one, he started listing out who, among his friends and fellow farmers, could help him. He stopped in the middle of the road when the thought of borrowing a horse carriage with a speedy horse occurred to him. *The hospital is far away, but God is merciful . . . God is merciful, Melang, you will arrive safely at the hospital.*

From afar, Tano could see his hut with all the lights on. The windows were open. A lantern was placed on the porch, its glow stretching out beyond their gate and lighting up the road in front of the hut.

Tano grew nervous. *Why are so many people here?*

He hurried his steps. As soon as he reached the door, everyone turned around to look at him. Tano could hear his heart beating fast. Had Melang given birth? His neighbours did not turn away. He slowly put his lantern down. From inside their house, an outcry broke the silence. *Melang has given birth!* He approached his wife. The floor was damp. The doctor came to him and said, 'I'm sorry, Tano.'

Tano knelt down beside Melang. Tears began streaming down his cheeks. He grabbed his wife's hand and nervously stared at her pale face. Within a few seconds, he wept uncontrollably, undeterred by his masculinity.

'We're lucky the baby came out alive,' the doctor said, 'otherwise . . .'

Melang's face was at peace, it seemed as if she was only sleeping. The tears Tano shed fell onto her chest.

'Such is life, Tano,' the doctor continued, 'you will have to learn to accept her death. It was probably just her time to go. Sooner or later, we will all reach the finish line, Tano. We have no idea when our time will come. Sometimes death comes without forewarning.'

From the crevices in the rooftop, raindrops were falling into the basin beside Melang. Outside, the drops from the showers could be seen suspended from the roof's edges. The raindrops fell slowly and gently, like teardrops falling onto one's cheek.

Melang's wake lasted for two nights. The farmers' wives were in charge of dressing and fixing her hair. With the help of his friend Nazario, Tano was able to sell his rice crops, and along with some donations, prepared for Melang's funeral.

At the back of their hut, a few farmers had gathered timber to build the coffin. The coffin was simple but with a glass in front of the face of the deceased.

The next day, they dug Melang's grave. Under the supervision of the midwife's husband, Hulyan, some men went downtown to talk to a priest. The cemetery was not open to the public, so they had to bury Melang's remains in a plot beside it. The spot was unoccupied, but they still needed to obtain a mayor's permit to use the public property. They wished to know if there were other options.

Tano pooled all the donations and his earnings from his previous harvest to pay for the mayor's permit. Together, the farmers started digging Melang's grave. They cut down all the cogon and wild grasses growing there. Almost the whole town came to pay their respects to Melang. The men wore formal polo shirts and cheap leather shoes, while the women wore their native blouses and skirts.

Tano remained speechless while his wife was being interred. Many noticed that he did not even cry when the men started shovelling the soil to cover the coffin. Tano remained beside his wife's grave until everyone had left. Melang occupied an isolated spot in one corner of the cemetery, where the bigger tombs of the more important and middle-class people were located. Some tombstones were made of marble, with a big cross on top. On others, there were statues of angels with their palms open, as if they were blessing the ashes of the deceased. Melang's had neither. Until her very last breath, she was enveloped in poverty.

'It's time to go, Tano,' Hulyan nudged Tano. They were the only ones left at the tomb. 'Let's go. We can come back again tomorrow.'

He held Tano's arm and they left Melang's grave. The ringing of church bells seemed to float in the air, as if reciting a prayer.

It was Ka Tindeng who breastfed Tano's child. If Ka Tindeng were not a robust woman, she would not have been able to breastfeed two babies at the same time. When it was time for the fiesta, both babies were baptized in the village. Tano's child was named Simon, while the midwife's son was named Duardo. They celebrated with a small feast at Ka Tindeng's house. Everyone was happy, except for Tano.

'Please enjoy yourself, Tano,' Hulyan told him. 'After all, it's your son's baptism today.'

In the midst of the celebration, it seemed as if Tano was still in shock. After the feast, he said goodbye and started to leave. When they asked him where he was going, he told them he was heading to the farm.

'Why are you leaving?' enquired Ka Tindeng. 'Stay here. Hulyan will accompany you tomorrow.'

But no one could stop Tano. He had changed a lot since the death of his beloved. He did not speak much, never made any plans for the future, and instead acted on impulse. He went back to his hut. He changed into his farming clothes and walked towards the fields.

'I feel sorry for Tano. I don't know what's bothering him.' Hulyan observed.

Ka Tindeng was resting against the wall as she breastfed the two babies. 'Did he proceed?'

'He did.'

'You know, Hulyan, I am worried. Did you see the look in Tano's eyes earlier? Oh Lord, he is acting strange.'

Since Melang died, Tano had been spending hours at the farm. He just visited his child occasionally, to check on him. If he was not at his hut, he was in the farm, planting crops. He seemed to watch his rice crops closely, waiting for them to mature and for the grains to be ready for harvest. Before the sun rose, he would have his back bent, planting his crops, making sure no space was left for water to run off. When the sun had risen, he would start removing the weeds. He would go home at noon time, cook his food, eat, and go back to the farm in the afternoon. After a long hard day at work, his muscles would be tired but he would not be able to sleep. Restless, he would rise from his bed, light the lamp, and rest his back against the open door while watching the darkness envelop the fields. His mind was preoccupied with a lot of things.

Sometimes, he would think of Pransiskong Mahirap (Wretched Francisco), the namesake of an old farmer from another village who lived miserably his whole life after his wife and child died. He lived alone, refusing to talk to anyone until he took his last breath. Tano also remembered Maestro Filemon, a former leader and teacher of the peasants, who was a deeply religious man. One evening, the townsfolk saw his body hanging from a tamarind tree. No one could understand why he had taken his own life when he knew it was against the laws of God. Pransiskong and Filemon were just two of his comrades who suffered tragic deaths. At this point, Tano could barely remember how each and every farmer had died because his mind was too muddled.

Tano had never felt so alone in his life. He was not sure if he would be able to face life's new challenges. Melang had meant the world to him, but life must go on. He must not give up because Baby Simon needed him.

At the back of his mind, Tano had a plan. He had brought his female carabao to the farm that had not given birth in such a long time that he suspected it had become barren. He wondered why the carabao's belly was protruding when he had hardly been able to feed her. It was then that he found out that the carabao was pregnant. He stopped making it work on the farm. He was always watching her— he lengthened her rope because otherwise the animal would not have been able to lie down when she gave birth; it would fall onto its knees.

One night, while he was lying on his bed, he heard his carabao moving about and groaning. He arose and carried a lantern outside. *She must be in labour*, he thought. He untied its rope and waited the whole night for her to give birth. The next morning, she birthed a calf.

He thought about how he could use the female carabao now that it had mothered a calf. One day, he went to town. He prepared swaddling clothes like Melang had prepared for their baby. He packed the baby's clothes in a native basket and went to see Ka Tindeng.

The midwife was flabbergasted at his request.

'I thought you were just visiting Simon,' said the midwife. 'Where are you taking him?'

'Tindeng is losing weight, Tano,' said Hulyan, 'our child is not getting enough milk. Nonetheless, we will take care of Simon like how your wife would have, if she were still alive. Don't be foolish. You can take the boy with you once he's a little older.'

But Tano insisted. He wouldn't leave without taking his son with him.

'Trust me, I can take care of his needs, Ka Tindeng,' Tano almost pleaded.

Ka Tindeng was teary-eyed; she did not know if she was feeling sorry for the baby or for Tano. Why was Tano taking away a baby who was just five months old?

'You'll just kill Simon, Tano,' Hulyan warned. 'Your son is not like a calf, who can feed on grass when it gets hungry.'

Tano shook his head. 'He is my son, Ka Tindeng. He belongs to me.'

'We're not saying Simon is not your child,' Hulyan calmly explained, still trying to understand Tano's intentions. 'We're just worried about his welfare. Will you please be reasonable? We could not care less if the boy was not yours.'

'Please listen, Tano,' agreed Ka Tindeng. 'You're just confused because Melang passed away recently. Please do not let the boy suffer.'

The midwife started to cry but Tano remained firm.

'I will take him, Ka Tindeng.'

Hulyan gave up and asked Ka Tindeng to hand over the sleeping Simon and his belongings to Tano.

'You are out of your mind, Tano,' Hulyan told him as he left their house.

'He is going to kill the boy, Hulyan,' was all Ka Tindeng could say as she rushed to the window to watch Tano leave.

From the midwife's hut, Tano proceeded to his house, carrying Simon. He grabbed the hammock that he had made from the roof. He placed the mat—which Melang had sewn—inside it like a sheet and carefully laid Simon on it. He opened his native bag containing the swaddling clothes, on top of which lay a feeding bottle.

That afternoon, the weather was cloudy. He had tied his carabao to a pole. He loaded the baby's things that he had prepared onto it and got on the carabao's back, riding with his left arm cradling the boy and his right hand wielding the whip.

The townspeople were shocked to see him carrying Simon. They had been wondering why Tano was always at the fields, and now here he was, and he had his baby with him.

'Where is he going?' asked one farmer.

Tano did not look at him.

'To the fields, I guess. After all, he brought his plow.'

'But why did he bring his boy?'

'Poor Tano has completely lost his mind!'

They watched Tano ride away to the fields. Some people from the village also stepped outside their huts to watch the farmer and his baby boy from the sidewalk. Tano just ignored them.

'Maybe he is going to live on the farm,' one farmer guessed.

'Tano is crazy if he thinks he can live on the farm. How will he feed his baby?'

'Maybe he will produce milk for his son. Let's just wait and see,' joked one of them.

Tano became the talk of the town for being foolish. Many thought he had gone crazy; they speculated that it all must have started when his wife passed away. Many were also scared that the baby might die of hunger. 'Good Lord!' exclaimed Mariang Basahan when he heard about the matter, 'I can only be thankful I have no child. Otherwise, Apolonio would starve our baby, too.' Mariang Basahan had always hoped for a child but the couple just kept on trying. Some folks said that out of desperation, Maria even tied layers of rags around her waist just to have a bump. Hence her nickname, Mariang Basahan (Maria Rags).

Tano built a new hut for his son and himself on the farm. The rooftop, made of cogon grass, also became a trellis for bottle gourd. In the backyard was a banana tree. The hut was beside a well, while a row of string beans served as a fence. It was four kilometres away from town, and one had to pass through a thicket of trees and plants. Before Melang passed away, while that lot was still unoccupied, it was full of snakes, but that did not scare Tano. He was sure he wouldn't allow the snakes to be the predators, but prey. More than ever, he needed privacy to carry out his plans while avoiding gossip.

Every morning, after the calf had finished suckling, Tano would drive it away and cover the nipple with a sharp twig from a guava tree to keep the calf at bay. Tano needed the milk of the carabao to feed baby Simon; the calf was still young but it could chew on grass to survive. When the calf grew older and the female carabao could no longer produce milk, Tano searched for a lactating goat. He saw one in a nearby village and bartered the goat for one sack of rice from the livestock farmer. The child who used to care for it, cried, and the goat likewise protested, but Tano needed the goat more.

When the goat could no longer produce milk, Tano fed Simon soft porridge. The boy was lanky and sickly before he could learn to walk. Ka Tindeng paid the boy a visit once and Tano thought she would take him away.

'He was being sarcastic. He actually sneered at me,' Ka Tindeng complained to Hulyan afterwards.

The farmers had stopped talking to Tano. They thought he had gone nuts, but they couldn't help but wonder about Tano's son. Was he still alive? Often, when they passed by

Tano's house, they could not help walking slowly. They waited to hear footsteps or a baby's cry—any noise that would indicate the baby was still alive—but they heard nothing.

'Crazy Tano is digging in his backyard,' some shepherds would say, 'he's probably burying his son.'

No one ever heard the baby cry when they passed by Tano's house. If only they knew Tano took his child with him everywhere he went, even to the fields, while he worked. Before he plowed, he erected two sturdy poles opposite each other in a corner in the fields. He then laid Simon in a hammock under a shady tree with two pillows on opposite sides to keep him secure. Whenever Tano heard the baby cry, he left his plow, gently swung the hammock, and fed his child.

The rainy days and summer came, followed by the planting and harvesting season. Little Simon miraculously survived and grew up. He had been thin and sickly as a baby, but once he left the hammock, started crawling on his knees and climbing up and down the hut, he grew into a healthy and robust little boy.

Simon had no toys, so Tano once again went to a nearby village to look for a puppy for him. The puppy became Simon's playmate, taking the place of kids of his own age. The puppy was his faithful companion, following him wherever he went, a toy and playmate, all rolled into one for the boy growing up on the farm.

'Is that Tano's son?' the farmers would remark in astonishment when they saw the boy playing with a puppy in front of their hut. 'It's a miracle he's survived!'

'I still wouldn't take any bets,' said one farmer. 'If an elderly person can die from negligence, what of a five-month-old? Take poor Isko, for instance, whose child passed away when he was only seven years old.'

'Comrade, desperate measures,' answered the farmer's friend. 'Look at Tano. He is such a resourceful parent.'

'Thank goodness,' shrieked Mariang Basahan, 'that Tano's child survived! But mothers always know what's best for their child.'

News of Simon's miraculous upbringing reached the whole village, and they could only admire Tano and feel relieved that he had been able to raise him alone. According to a few witnesses, Simon was a dark-skinned boy with thick brown hair, who wore no underpants and was always greasy.

'Who would bathe him?' one mother asked, 'We only ever see him playing with a dog.'

'A dog?' The children laughed in amusement.

'He would not have died,' an old woman remarked, 'Didn't you notice the soft spot on his skull throbbing when he was born? That was a sign that resilient blood was coursing through his veins.'

Once again, it rained and the summer season came, along with the planting and harvesting seasons, and Simon—who wore no underpants and was not allowed to step beyond the fence—could now be seen riding the back of a carabao, watching over the fields. He wore his father's huge, torn native hat, which almost covered his eyes, chewing on a strand of grass as he rode along. When his father called out to him, 'Simoonn, ho, Simoonnn!', he would answer, shouting, 'I'm coming!'

In 1901, the Americans established the civil government in the Philippines. Military governors were replaced by one senior civilian governor. Right from the start, the Philippines had asked for independence—after all, it was what they had been promised. The change in administration was followed by the adoption of the Jones Act, establishing a new legislature, consisting of Filipino members.

A new mission was established under Quezon's chair.

Tano had little idea of what was going on. From the very beginning, he had never showed any interest in politics. The same was true for other peasants. They had no control over who ruled the country and they had somehow managed their expectations. They grew up dependent on the authorities to decide for them. They were given importance only during elections, when the electoral candidates would resort to all kinds of means and propaganda to win their votes.

Now age was catching up to Tano. He had started sprouting grey hair on his head, his skin was starting to wrinkle, and he was losing a lot of weight. One afternoon, Tano dug a huge hole in their backyard to bury his female carabao. Its calf assisted him in his effort—the same calf that had competed with Simon for its mother's milk.

'Good Lord, the animal gave up on Tano,' the farmers said upon learning about the carabao's death. 'A time will come when Tano himself will surrender.'

But on the contrary, Tano was not planning to give up, though oftentimes, he had to ask Simon to rub oil on his body before going to bed. 'Please rub oil on my back. It's aching,' he would say before lying down on a mat and feeling the smooth oil spread onto his shoulders, Simon's little fingers massaging his aching muscles.

One day in June, when Tano went downtown, he bought new clothes for eight-year-old Simon. He called out to his son, who was just returning home from the fields. Simon was pleasantly surprised. He raised his arms to put them on and pressed them down neatly onto his body.

'They fit perfectly, Father,' Simon said as he looked at himself in the mirror. 'What's the occasion?'

Tano fished out a pair of slippers from his trouser pocket. He slid them onto Simon's feet. 'You will go to school, Simon.'

'Will I, Father?' Simon jumped with joy, 'I will go to school! I will go to school!'

The next Monday, Tano and Simon went downtown together. Tano was wearing his only white trousers, which had turned slightly brown from being stowed away inside a chest for a long time. Simon, who had just had a haircut at the hands of his father, wore his new clothes. Their hair was shining with pomade made from coconut oil.

*You will go to school, Simon,* Tano thought as he glanced at his son. *You will go to school!*

Tano had taught himself to read using spelling books for beginners. But before he could learn to write, his father stopped sending him to school and instead asked him to help out at the farm. His father insisted that farming could never be learned at school, only from experience. But Tano did not want to be like the rest of the farmers in the village, who, once their children had learned how to read and write, would then teach them how to plow, until they, too, had become slaves to the farm. He had personally witnessed his parents becoming slaves to the farm and he did not want Simon to meet the same fate. Paterno Borja had taught him an important lesson the night he had refused to lend him his car.

On 29 March 1899, the Spaniards established San Roque (Isidro) as the capital of the Philippines. One could find big houses here; it was where the wealthiest of the town lived, and it extended throughout the eight provinces.

Most of the old Spanish houses were built beside the river. The Pampanga River was the means of commercial transportation during that time. Boats loaded with goods and freight would travel down the river, carrying passengers who were leaving San Roque for greener pastures. For covering shorter distances, poorer folks often used domesticated animals to pull their wagons.

One could spot the old camarín beside the river, alongside ruins of big warehouses, where tobacco was once stored. San Roque was among the eight towns that enjoyed a monopoly over the tobacco trade during the Spanish era. Even now, one can see the abandoned ruins of the old camarín, made of bricks.

Also at the riverbank were thick and high walls that served as defenses against the bandits who terrorized the town. One can only find a few historical ruins left behind now; the barricades were broken down for building stairwells or maybe a water fountain. Allegedly, these walls were built by bonded labour.

From the series of huge houses beside the river, Captain Martin's house stood out—he was one of the richest Filipinos in San Roque. The compound used to serve as a prison for the Filipinos who rebelled against the Spaniards. It was believed that there still lay skeletons buried in the dark corners of the former prison, which was now owned by the heirs of the Captain, including madams of high stature.

The galvanized roof was broad, the windows were made of *capiz*, and the floors were laid with thick and tight screws. Lanterns lit up the huge hall, which was apparently the receiving chambers for Spaniards and wealthy Filipino guests. The entrance door seemed to be as enormous as that of the church; the floors were made of marble, and upon going inside, one saw the garage holding an ancient carriage that had once roved the streets of San Roque proudly.

The house needed some repairs—the roof leaked when it rained; there were crevices in the walls, probably due to strong earthquakes—but overall, the mansion had stood the test of time. It still stood out from all the rest of the mansions, although when night fell, crawling scorpions, croaking geckos, and flying bats came to occupy the abandoned house.

The Captain's house was almost right across from Isauro Regente's mansion, a Spaniard who had arrived in the Philippines and claimed a high position he had probably been denied in his own country. He likewise owned an ancestral house and wished to preserve its architecture. Isauro's house was surrounded by high and thick fences. His expansive field employed quite a number of farmers who sold their crops during harvest season, one of whom was Tano.

In the heart of San Roque stood the old quarters of general and civil guards, which now served as a school.

In the plaza were the general's quarters who had proudly captured bandits when they had attempted to overthrow the brave general of the Spanish government, waving the black flag bearing a white cross of bones and a skull.

There were big houses that stood at the edge of the plaza. One of them belonged to Paterno Borja, a feudal lord of San Roque. This house was not originally owned by the Borjas. It had been bought by a Spaniard named Don Segundo, who had held a high position in the government, during the Spanish occupation. Don Segundo had married a Filipina, whose surname was Borja. She came from a poor family. Upon Don Segundo's death, he transferred his house to his wife, leaving her in charge of their businesses. The Filipina was able to acquire a large hectare of land in San Roque, which was later converted into a rice field.

Borja's house towered over the villages below, and Simon would gaze at it while growing up. A woman in fashionable clothes could be seen descending the stairs and coming out of the steel gates, holding a little boy. The boy had a fair and smooth complexion, smelled fresh, wore shiny shoes and new clothes.

'He's also going to school, Father,' Simon observed, following his father, pointing his finger at the little boy.

Tano knew the little boy. He was Borja's youngest child. The boy's baptism had been celebrated with a lavish feast at the Borja residence—he was a year older than Simon. During the baptism, he had seen Borja's car leaving their house to pick up and drop their guests to their homes. Owning a car was a status symbol in San Roque, and many wished they could ride in that car, too.

It was the same car that Tano had been denied on the night when Simon was born, and Melang had died.

Simon met many children at school. At the entrance, he saw a little girl with her long hair tied with a ribbon. She was fair-skinned and was accompanied by a woman holding an umbrella for her.

Tano knew the little girl as well. She was the youngest child of Isauro Regente. Simon had never seen anyone as pretty as her; to him, she was like an angel. The woman holding the umbrella was her mother. Everyone knew Regente loved his children dearly, but did not extend the same treatment to his Filipina wife.

At school, before Simon registered, Tano saw Ka Tindeng and Nazario.

'Simon!' Ka Tindeng exclaimed as she saw the boy holding Tano's hand.

She had not seen Simon in a long time—ever since the day Tano had seemed suspicious that she had come to take his son away from him—but a mother's heart could never forget the baby she had nursed. Ka Tindeng, too, had grey hair now, and the wrinkles were carved deeply into her forehead.

Simon held onto his father's arm tightly, trying to figure out the identity of this woman who had called out to him and was now approaching him.

Ka Tindeng tried to hold Simon's shoulders, but he shrank away from her. She became teary-eyed. 'My baby has grown up, Tano,' she said, still gazing at Simon. 'My child has grown up!'

Tano was touched by Ka Tindeng's maternal instincts. There was a long silence, after which she called out to a boy who was as old as Simon. He was also dark-skinned and wore slippers; he seemed shy.

'This is Duardo,' Ka Tindeng introduced her son. 'You two are brothers.'

*Brothers?* The two boys looked at each other for a while.

'I breastfed you both at the same time,' explained Ka Tindeng.

The two boys hung their heads—how were they finding out about this only now?!

'And this is Salvador,' Nazario smiled as he introduced the boy he was holding, who seemed like he was in a higher grade.

'You will all go to school today,' Ka Tindeng mused, smiling. 'I assume that Duardo and Simon,' she bent and looked at Simon in the eye, 'you two are classmates. Don't fight, okay?' She smiled as she turned to look at her son. 'Duardo, come here. Share your snacks with Simon.'

While Ka Tindeng was talking to Duardo and Simon, Nazario turned towards Tano. He marvelled at how suddenly Simon seemed to have grown up fast.

'It seems like yesterday!' he exclaimed, referring to the day when Tano had taken Simon to the farm for the first time.

Tano could only smile in agreement.

For Simon, everything seemed like a mystery. At the farm, he had no other companion but his father; no other playmate but his dog. Now here were two little boys, one of whom was offering him a rice cake. He was beginning to feel a little excited; he looked up at the woman who had been holding him by his shoulders until then.

Simon's classes were during daytime. Tano would take him to school before he went to the farm and Simon would go home by himself upon class dismissal. Simon would join Tano in the farm later during the day.

Tano would wait with cooked rice for Simon to come home. His lunch would be wrapped in banana leaves, since he could not come home during lunchtime. He ate his lunch at school, sharing his food with Duardo and Ador, who also brought their own packed lunches from home. In the afternoon, while returning from school, Simon would once again take the carabao to the farm. While riding the carabao, his shoulders in sync with the steps of the animal, he would sing or whistle a tune he had learned at school:

'I've never seen a big apple,
A big apple, a big apple . . .'

Simon knew how to whistle from a very young age—and sometimes, when he would find a thicket of grass, he would untie the carabao and let it graze. He would spread the sack on the ground and lay on it himself, chewing on any strand of grass he could find. He would cross his legs, feeling the earth breathe underneath him, staring at the shape of the clouds and imagining what they could be. Sometimes, instead of lying on the ground, he would sleep on the carabao's back.

Tano was amused at Simon's diligence towards his studies. Some nights, while he rested, he would hear him reading aloud beside a burning lamp. Simon would be lying prone with a book in front of him. At other times, when Tano came home from fishing, he would hear his son speaking to himself in a modulated voice, trying to recall what he had learned and practising public speaking. When Simon was not yet fast asleep, Tano would smile to himself, as he silently observed Simon taking his studies seriously. Sure enough, each day, upon crossing their doorstep, Tano would find Simon in a prone position, reading a book; sometimes, the boy would not even notice his arrival.

The father and son shared wonderful moments together when they were all alone, with nobody else in the fields. One Saturday afternoon, a shepherd passing by their house saw both of them wrestling. Tano had challenged Simon. They were both shouting and laughing, rolling around in the grass. The young shepherd returned to the village and told everyone what he had witnessed. Many laughed like they could not believe him.

'It is true!' the shepherd exclaimed. 'I swear I am telling the truth.'

The townsfolk shrugged their shoulders and told the boy anything was possible. Tano could act crazy sometimes. If they were in his shoes, however, they would not wrestle with their child.

Simon always brought news to his father when he came home from school. Tano would hear the different things and feel sad, unless it was about how his son was getting good grades. Simon would tell him, for example, that their teachers showed favouritism towards Alejandro Borja, even though he was not that smart, and he'd ask why he was included in the honour roll and all of the school's programmes, 'How come, Father?'

Tano could not tell him the real reason: it was because he came from a rich family.

'Elena Regente seems nice,' Simon would tell Tano, and before his father could ask about her, he would remember that she was the Spaniard's daughter, even though 'the little angel' was his son's classmate.

Simon also mentioned Ador.

'Ador is in the honour roll among grade-five students, Father. He participates in our school's contests, too.'

'Follow Ador's example,' Tano would tell him.

And so Simon continued to take the bumpy road to his school. He travelled a long way, but his determination to continue with his studies was unstoppable. He set off alone before the sun rose and had no companion on his way home at sunset.

Planting and harvesting schedules were marked on a farmer's calendar by instinct. Somehow, they could predict exactly when the rains and summer would arrive, and they would be prepared. During lean months, while waiting for the seedlings to germinate, farmers would attend to their livestock, which was usually their other source of income.

The farmers marked the grain according to quality. They would get the next set of seedlings only from the best grains, so Tano would bring home a bundle of the best grains and proudly tell those he met that they were his harvest.

One night, the wind was unusually cold. The weather was chilly and the farmers' children hid and covered themselves with their thin, pauper blankets. Tano was sound asleep. When he awoke and gazed outside his window, the sky was cloudy. The farmers going to the fields seemed to have predicted the weather and had already warmed themselves by cooking fires or burned heaps of dry leaves. In San Roque, during the cold months, some farmers would make a bonfire along the road to warm themselves up before setting off for work.

Red ants had started to swarm the rice fields. In their mouths were leftover grains. Quite a number of these soldier ants gathered their food from the rice fields and marched towards their queen's sanctuary, storing up food in preparation for inclement weather.

The carabao stood at the riverbank. It bent its knees slightly to drink water; its gentle eyes seemed to be staring into the distance. It would point its nose upwards as if to taste the wind, then it would remove its soiled hooves from the river.

The whole sky was suddenly covered by a blanket of dark clouds. Small, brown swallows were swiftly migrating towards the opposite direction.

Last night, inside their small hut, Tano had heard the wind blowing and the heavy downpour of the rain.

'There's a storm, Father,' the awakened Simon had said. He had been lying on his bed with his blanket up to his neck.

The wind was trying to force its way through their door. The draughts from the windows were playing with Tano's grey hair. The storm was like an intruder trying to barge into their house. Every person owns a door in his character that he guards against intruders in order to feel more secure. From the rear window, Tano could see the rice fields being flooded. Layers of grain were being swept away by the harsh wind and rain. How could his raincoat save his crops? Was it strong enough to cover him and save his crops?

It seemed as if the typhoon only took a vacation to regain its strength—once it had recuperated, it would return to its devastating business, greedier than ever. The stems of the grains did not fight the storm, they surrendered themselves to the call of nature. Once one surrenders, one is defeated and can no longer choose their death.

Tano remembered it had been raining on that night as well. Bolts of lightning were falling on the ground. That very night, there was a victim who met her end. Without a doubt, rain was needed, but not the kind that was destructive. Instead, light showers were needed to cool the earth.

'We need to harvest the rice, Simon,' Tano told his son. He was not too sure if he was making the right decision. The years of toil had brought him as close to his own grave as the crops he had planted. 'We need to harvest our rice, Simon. Otherwise there will be no grain left to harvest.'

The hut's door was flung open by the wind—Tano could now see his grain drowning in the flood. He felt an unusual pain, like a rat being pierced by a cat with its sharp claws before being devoured. It was the pain brought on by the typhoon—the one that was destroying the crops he had toiled away for, pouring his blood, sweat, and tears into rearing them, only to be too helpless to save them from destruction.

'What will become of our grains, Father?' Simon asked with apprehension. He had helped his father plow the fields and, like him, the storm had crushed his spirit, too.

Tano did not reply. He sat in a corner, resting his head against the wall. He lifted his wrinkled kneecap and placed his veiny hand on top of it. He began to worry once more if he would be able to save his crops—there might still be some left—but could the remaining crops withstand another typhoon? In the last few years, he had become increasingly paranoid about being blindsided by the unforeseen. The destructive typhoon had come from the south of Sierra Madre. What if another typhoon followed from the north? The farmers were scheduled to harvest their rice three days from now, but the typhoon has foiled their plans.

Tano remembered the time the swarms of locusts had infested the fields of San Roque. He had been as young as Simon then. The large number of locusts had turned the sky black; they had left nothing of their crops but skeletons of stems. Something had to be done to save the farmers' crops. The next morning, the president of the village had suggested that the townsfolk eat the locusts. Tano wanted to have his share. They built a well in the farm and the locusts jumped into it. The farmers then lifted the dead locusts by sackfuls. They were sold at the market by the kilo or cup.

Tano also remembered the first time he had seen crows in San Roque. They used to grow corn and the birds would often eat them, which was why he had placed a scarecrow in the middle of the farm. The rest of the farmers also followed his example, until one day, a hunter spotted the crows, and with a single shot, was able to gun down seventeen birds that fell to the ground.

The crows and locusts had vanished. But nothing had been able to stop the heavy downpour in his lifetime.

'Let's harvest the rice, Simon,' Tano said as the dawn broke. He was holding his son's arm.

'There's a storm, Father.'

'No rice will be left because the rain will not stop. Come.'

Simon had no choice but to concede. They proceeded to the porch to get their work clothes. Tano led the way. They were both wearing wide-rimmed hats. Tano handed Simon two lanterns stored under a dusty table. He grabbed bundles of rope that were not yet soaked and cleaned but would do the job.

'Let's go.'

Tano opened the door. He was greeted by the strong winds and harsh rain. His working clothes were immediately soaked and started clinging to his body.

Almost all the string beans in front of their hut had collapsed. The bottle gourd had been swept off the roof. In the backyard, the banana tree had fallen.

Tano went towards the fields. He held the rim of his native hat that was being swept by the wind. He could hardly keep his balance. He and Simon went to a spot with the most grains remaining.

'Work on this area while I work on the other side,' he instructed Simon as he held the lantern.

Tano grabbed handfuls of the grain. He was more skilled than Simon, who was still a novice. They continued with the harvest. Simon's fingers started to swell up. He was getting cold. The cold air was spreading down his nape and back as he continued to bend; the native hat could no longer keep his hair dry.

Simon looked at his father. His native hat had been blown off into the flooded rice fields. Tano removed his raincoat; it was obstructing his movements. They had to move quickly.

Simon bent once again, looking for germinating seedlings. He tried to grab as many as he could. Why did they have to harvest the grain in the midst of a storm? His father's behaviour confused him. His hand jerked as he felt a sharp pain on his thumb. He dropped the seedlings. He looked at his palm and noticed that the nail on his left thumb was chipped. He watched his thumb bleed and his hands shook as he held his cut thumb. He sucked the blood from his thumb. His felt a sharp tingling spreading throughout his jaw. For a while he was delirious, but Tano paid no attention.

Simon went back to their hut. He held his wounded thumb under running water from the faucet and then covered it with gauze. The cold weather stopped the bleeding immediately. While wrapping the bandage around his thumb, he stared outside their hut. His father was still engrossed in harvesting the rice.

He felt sorry for his father. He was certain that he was feeling cold, too, but then why wasn't he stopping? Would saving the crops be worth it in comparison to the repercussions the reaping would have on his health?

'Father, come back!'

Tano did not answer. Did he even hear Simon?

When Tano ignored him, Simon did not call his father anymore.

It was already noontime when Tano returned to their hut. The rag at their doorstep was soaking wet. Tano emptied his pockets of the grain he was able to save, then immediately changed into dry clothes.

'Drink this ginger tea,' offered Simon. Tano's hands shook as he drank from the cup. After drinking the tea, he grabbed a blanket and draped it on his back. He laid down on the bamboo bed and lit the lamp.

It was still raining until later that night, and Tano was burning with fever. He tried to move, raising his arm.

'We will harvest rice again tomorrow, Simon,' it was already late, but he still reminded his son who was watching over beside him. 'Or else we will have no harvest.'

As Tano feared, the typhoon from the north followed the one from the south. The strong winds once again swept his farm. Tano could not sleep, still worried about his crops.

'Simon, we cannot waste any time,' he told his son. 'Come, let's get back to work.'

That typhoon brought back painful memories for Tano. Not only was he coughing incessantly now—it was already summer, and his coughing refused to get better—but rather every night, he feared another storm would come and cause more destruction.

'Tano will never give up on his farm animals,' said one farmer when Tano took care of his female carabao for the longest time. 'But he stands no chance against the typhoon.'

Tano was one of the most hardworking farmers in their village. Pidyong was strong—he could carry six sacks of rice at once—but ever since a mango tree trunk had fallen on his legs, he had been paralyzed. Earlier, Tano could out-drink all the men who sat drinking from bamboo mugs—he would not give up until there was nothing more left of the ginger beer. He was like Saro, who could build the biggest bonfire and could split a bamboo branch in half with his bare hands. But now, even Saro had grown weaker ever since the day he had vomited blood.

One night, while lying on their bamboo bed, Tano whispered to his son: 'We will go back to our old house.'

Simon could not reply and lay staring at his father.

'We will return.'

Simon could not figure out why they were going back to their old house, all of a sudden. His heart skipped a little beat. He longed to have a home in the village so much, he always wished to go and live closer to Duardo and Ador, but his father clearly had other reasons, which he was afraid to ask.

Simon heard Tano's dry cough as his father's head rested against the opened door of the hut; the cool wind playing with the grey hair on his forehead. *It's cold there, Father*, Simon wished to tell him, but he'd rather not speak.

'Your father is old now, Simon,' an old farmer had once told him when he had come for a glass of water during his break from labour. 'But when he was younger, my Simon, he was the best farmer of all. He would work overtime in the fields all the time.'

'My Simon,' the farmer had continued, 'you were still a baby when Tano first brought you here. You were still being breastfed. But now that your father is old, I'm sure that you will go back to live in the village. You will return, Simon, I am telling you. Has anyone told you that one always misses their home?'

Simon stared at his father once again. *We will return home, Father?* He was begging for an answer. But his father was now fast asleep—his feet extended, his seemingly bruised shoulders resting and his limbs lying lifeless on the ground. Tano's palms were open; it seemed as if he would never close them to fight again.

Simon wanted to cry. Now that his father was fast asleep, he felt so alone. He wanted to get up, wake his father and tell him, 'Father, I've laid the mat out for you,' but he could not move or speak a word. He did not wish to disturb his slumber, knowing he'd been drained and exhausted for so long now.

The next afternoon, Tano and Simon prepared to return to their home in the village. They loaded their bags into the carabao carriage. Simon followed Tano, their shadows reflected on the path as they travelled. The carabao started treading the road slowly. They were finally going home to be reunited with old friends; to the turning point in Tano's life.

# Part II

## Escape

## 1942

It was during the height of World War II that Tano and Simon went back to their old house.

No one knew they were coming—except for Duardo—but on the breeze blowing in, the news travelled, spreading like wildfire throughout the neighbourhood. That afternoon, the greasy children stopped playing, a look of wonder on their faces; the flocks, shepherds, and farmers halted at the sight of Tano and Simon arriving. They had returned to their old home. The elderly farmers greeted them warmly.

Darkness had fallen and the lamps in the huts were lit. The housewives started lighting the stoves to prepare the family's supper. They shared bedtime stories about the life of St Isidro Labrador as they lay beside their children, telling them how the angels had helped Isidro the farmer. Isidro did not work on Sundays, and was mocked and called lazy. One Sunday, when all other farmers had left for the farm, they were shocked to see angels plowing and digging in the fields. Since then, they stopped making fun of Isidro and decided to treat the Sabbath as holy, worshipping him as the Blessed One.

Tano's hut had been abandoned for the longest time—ever since Melang had died. When they arrived, however, after Simon lit the lamp, its flicker was still somehow able to dispel the darkness. That tiny flickering flame was enough for Tano to assess the hut's damages and the repairs and renovations required to make it inhabitable again.

Their initial days in the village were spent renovating their hut: the holes in the rooftop made of palm leaves were filled in with plaster; the cracked stairs and floors were replaced; they even fixed the carabao's pen. They cut down the tall grass that had grown over time and burned it, then cut bamboo trunks to replace their worn-out fences.

Tano continued to plow the farm while Simon went to school. Simon would help his father out only on the weekends. He was now a regular student and had also learned the ropes of farming. Among the three friends—Duardo, Ador, and he—only he and Ador were able to finish high school. Ador later moved to Manila, where he pursued further education.

During this time, President Quezon had launched his social justice programme. In a nearby town in San Miguel, a master had killed his housemaid—the daughter of a farmer—and buried her in their backyard. The president personally oversaw the investigations into this matter and was able to win the sympathy of the townspeople. During a speech at the San Roque Plaza, he spoke of equality amongst people—the farmers and their landlords. Tano only wished he could have heard Quezon's speech because he wanted to know what was in store for peasants like him and their next generation.

Aside from the president, there were other prominent people who gave speeches at the plaza. They all spoke in fluent Tagalog. They tried to unite the workers in the city and the farmers in the rural areas. Tano was able to witness the speech made by one such great orator, who said, 'no one is born a slave, it is colonialism that brought in slavery, which has lasted for more than three hundred years. Three hundred years and nothing has changed. We need to break the *cadena perpetua*; we needed to unite to attain the goal of equality.'

Tano later learned that the great orator's companions had been kidnapped in Manila. From then on, no speeches were held at the plaza, but their movements and agendas managed to reach far-flung areas and even the farms. When the great orator's companions were released, Tano witnessed a few more men crop up, who made lofty promises to the farmers.

The global war had a debilitating effect on the economy. Salaried workers could no longer keep up with the rising prices of basic commodities. Businesses were going bankrupt because people no longer had any purchasing power.

To address the widespread recession, the United States promised to create jobs that were relevant to the times and would likewise respond to the needs of the growing population. To start off, English was made part of the curriculum in schools. Schools also offered other courses that would help students acquire skills and training to find or generate employment.

As he grew up, Simon became much taller than Tano, but he inherited his father's brown complexion and stature. He was quite intelligent, but he could never earn honours in school because he didn't belong to an influential family; his teachers refused to acknowledge merit in poor farmers like him.

Elena had been Simon's classmate since he had started school, and was the youngest child of their landlord. The daughter was entirely unlike her condescending father. She had a Caucasian complexion, long hair, and no matter how tired she got at school, would still manage to smile. Simon felt her soft palms; she had long eyelashes that were so alluring. And above all, she had a big heart.

One night, Tano learned that his son was going on a date with Elena at the plaza, but had kept it a secret from him. As Simon was looking at himself in the mirror, wearing his best clothes, trying to look his best, he probed, 'Where are you going, Simon?'

Lately, Tano wanted to know all about his son's plans all the time.

'Duardo and I are just going downtown, Father. We will be home early.'

'Don't go.'

Simon was surprised at Tano's reply.

'We won't take long, Father.'

'Are you meeting up with Elena?'

How did his father know? Did someone tell him? No one in school knew he was courting Elena. Could it have been Duardo?

'Stay away from her,' Tano warned, without looking at his son.

'Father . . .'

'Don't deny it, Simon.'

Simon remembered what had happened when they were together in the fields, the previous day. One of Regente's servants had approached Tano, saying the master was calling him. Simon was apprehensive, though he was certain it would only be about the harvest.

'End your relationship with her, Simon.'

End their relationship? Simon was hurt. It was the first time Simon was in love and now his father wanted him to end it. He descended the stairs with his head hanging low. From their bamboo bed, Tano could hear his son talking to Duardo. He had to stop his son for good reason.

Regente had been sitting beside the window when Tano had arrived. Tano had removed his slippers before entering their house. He had held his native hat as he had entered the living room and greeted the Spaniard.

'You called for me, sir?'

The Spaniard stood up and shook his head.

'It's terrible, Tano, you would never suspect what a foolish thing your son is doing. Look at this.' The Spaniard showed him a few letters. Tano took them. He realized they were one of the reasons why Simon stayed up late at nights.

'If I had learned of this sooner, I would have sent Elena to Concordia to study. Please ask your son to stop courting her.'

Tano could feel himself shrinking with embarrassment. He wished to protest but Regente had irrefutable evidence and was clearly telling the truth. He walked slowly towards home. *Why was this urgent for Regente?* He chided himself for behaving like a docile lamb in front of the Spaniard. Regente was so good in giving advice. His words were not bluntly offensive. He was his landlord and so he was afraid to talk back. You should never try to reason with your landlord.

The harvest season arrived and the farmers set off for their fields once again. They came early in the morning to reap their harvests. They were having a good time; the gentlemen chaperoning the meek young ladies. Later, the men would ask these ladies if they could join them for lunch.

Once the rice had been reaped, the grain was placed in big, round native plates and laid out in the sun to dry. The farmers hurriedly laid them out across the road, side by side, laying as many plates as they could to ensure good profits. Women and children sometimes joined them, carrying baskets full of rice grains they had collected. Once their containers were full, they would proceed to the rice mill. After painstakingly winnowing the grain, they would lay the milled rice out on sacks spread on the ground to dry.

There were small convenience stores near the rice mill. At night, the stores would be very busy. Young farmers could be see bartering pails and pails of rice for cigarettes, beer, and any other drinks the ladies were selling. While milling the rice, men and women would sing love songs in chorus. The smoke from the rice mill gradually diminished. The machine spouted the rice out, forming heaps of grain that was ready to sell.

After the farmers had received their shares from the landlord, they would go on to gather fresh grass to feed their tired carabaos.

Whenever Simon had the chance, he would attend to farming and polishing the rice grains. He would join in the farmers' songs as they planted and harvested. Although he had lived on the farm his entire life, school had opened up a whole new world to him.

He had started avoiding Elena, but they inevitably managed to bump into each other. Elena was more beautiful than ever. She had a subdued face, yet her eyes still sparkled. One time, when they crossed paths, she smiled first and he wondered why she was still being nice to him, even though he was giving her the silent treatment.

Tano had grown even thinner and his coughing bouts more frequent. Simon would apply crushed ginger all over his back to somehow soothe his tired muscles. However, on chilly days and during cold months, Tano would be forced to sit up and cough. He was worried he might be sick, but he could not care less. If he could not sleep, he would try to entertain himself by stepping out of the hut at night. He would sit on a bamboo bench and start sharpening his bolo. Beside the bamboo bench was the camachile tree to which he tied his carabao. On some nights, he would sit in front of a termite hill, which seemed to listen patiently to his woes.

'He cannot sleep, that's why he keeps his hands occupied,' explained Hulyan to his enquiring neighbours.

'He has always been like that,' Simon said; he could only agree with the farmers who wondered at Tano's ways.

One morning, as the farmers were plowing their fields, Tano went to the fields after sharpening his bolo. The farmers were not required to work quickly but he was eager to work. Simon was at school. Before long, Tano was riding his carabao, which was pulling his carriage with a metal plow mounted on the top. He was dressed in his working clothes. Their dog was leading the way.

On his way to the farm, Tano saw Masyong, a retired farmer. Masyong was not going to plow his fields because he had been keeping sick lately. Since sunrise, he would sit outside his home and sunbathe, as if the sun's rays could cure him or make him feel better.

'You're early, Tano,' greeted Masyong. His voice was sore. His eyes were bloodshot and his beard had grown long. Masyong's complexion had turned grey, like wilted grass lying crushed under a huge rock for years.

'How's your sunbathing going?' asked Tano.

Masyong could only smile and Tano felt like he was being impolite. But Masyong took no offence. How come it seemed as if Masyong never got any better? Aside from his sunbathing therapy, he also drank his own urine believing the nutrients from his body would be washed away from his urine.

'I will go back to work once I feel better,' Masyong would tell his fellow farmers. But he was not getting better and his wife and grown-up son also seemed to have been infected by the same disease as him. Masyong all the more continued drinking his own urine upon learning this is the secret steroid of muscular men in their village. Moreover, they would often see Masyong's wife collecting snails at the farm after he found out that snails tasted good with rice.

Tano suddenly found himself thinking about Masyong. Maybe he felt sorry for him, but he could also see himself in Masyong's shoes: once in their lives, they both had the vitality and vigour of youth, but even the strongest of men could not fight against age. Once Masyong had had a spat with his neighbour farmer, who was jealous of Masyong because his house was bigger. To get even with him, the neighbour had grabbed a handful of dry leaves and attempted to set his own house on fire in order to spread the fire to Masyong's house as well. Tano and Masyong were once in the prime of their lives, but life was full of surprises that were beyond their control, and sometimes good friends also turned into enemies.

The sun was at its peak and Tano's back and shoulders seemed to be burning. When he and the carabao turned to go home, he felt dizzy and could hardly breathe. His vision had dimmed; he could barely make out the large figure of his carabao. He fell onto his knees before collapsing on the ground. He massaged his chest. What was going on with him? His vision continued to blur but he could not pass out in the field. He tried to stand up but his knees shook violently. He set aside the plow somehow and whipped the carabao until they had slowly reached their hut. While untying the carabao, Tano could hardly maintain his balance, sweating profusely and coughing persistently. He knelt down and his native hat fell off; he forced himself to stand up—he had to climb up the steps of the hut, but he was already breathless and collapsed in front of his plow.

Only half of Tano's body was in the shade. His dark, wrinkled, and slender legs lay exposed in the sun. He had fallen into the mud in front of his plow. His almost hairless head was wet with sweat. He was breathless. The nerves in his neck were popping. He continued to cough as he lifted his pale face off the ground. In front of him, something red fell onto the ground. Trembling in fear, he touched it with his finger. He recited a short prayer, pleading with God as he placed his finger on his lips and licked it. *Blood!* In front of him was splattered his own blood. He had vomited blood. He coughed again and more blood spilled out in front of him. He closed his eyes and tears streamed from his deep-set eyes.

'Simon cannot know about this,' he whispered to himself. 'No one can know. I will not tell anyone.'

Tano was startled. He had to prop himself on his palms to prevent another fall—he stared at the blood that was spilling out of him. 'I will not tell anyone. I will not tell Simon. Dear God, Dear God . . .' He looked around but saw no one. Using his right hand, he started to dig, his nails scratching the ground. Dig. Dig. 'No one should know about this. I will not tell anyone.' Once he was able to dig a small pit, he started covering the blood with soil.

He then collapsed. When he regained consciousness, he slowly stood up. His shadow was crawling, too. He strained his legs to climb up the stairs to his hut. He felt he would collapse if he did not hold onto the stairs, as he made his way up like a wounded victim of war, sweat soaking his shirt. He fell near the doorstep. He called out for Simon; he called out for God.

Their loyal dog rushed to his side. After wandering outside for some time, the dog was returning to their hut, looking for his master when he smelled Tano lying by the stairs. He was lying beside his plow and the dog sniffed him. It then dug up the pit Tano had made to cover up the blood. Lowering its head and with its tail hanging, it sat down beside Tano, raised its head and let out a long, sad howl.

Somehow making his way into their hut, Tano had changed his clothes and laid down on the bamboo bed before Simon came home from school.

'You're not feeling well, Father?'

Tano gently nodded his head. Simon changed his clothes. He fetched water for them and then cooked their supper. Afterwards, he lit the lamp and approached his father. 'Let's eat, Father.'

Tano shook his head.

'The rice will get cold.'

'Go on and eat. I will eat later.'

Simon went back to the table and ate by himself. He occasionally glanced at his father. He started to wonder what was wrong. It was the first time his father was not joining him for supper; even when he was tired, he would find a way to get out of bed and come to eat. His father often reminded him not to skip meals; that when you were hungry, you should sprinkle salt on steamed rice and eat, so your stomach doesn't remain empty. Tano had no appetite that evening. Instead, he coughed continuously.

When he had finished his meal, Simon cleared the table and washed the dishes in the sink. He stepped outside and fed the carabao fresh grass. He could still hear his father coughing, so he stopped feeding the carabao and went in to check on him. Tano was sitting up on the bamboo bed. Simon gently massaged his back but when he spotted Tano's palms, he was startled to see blood.

Tano felt cold. His head was hanging low, his left arm resting on the bamboo bed.

'You shouldn't have plowed the fields,' Simon told his father.

Without Tano's knowledge, Simon took stock of their harvested crops that night. He sold their crops the following day, and fetched the doctor. The doctor vaccinated Tano and prescribed medicines, advising Tano to take complete rest.

'He shouldn't be doing heavy labour,' the doctor advised. 'Otherwise his condition will get worse. Is this the first time he has felt ill?'

As always, Duardo was the first to know about the condition of Simon's father. He slept over at their house, that night. Once Tano was fast asleep, the two friends started talking.

'I think I will stop my studies,' said Simon. 'Father is sick and there is no one to take care of him. We need to replenish our stock of rice.'

'Finish your studies,' suggested Duardo. 'I can help you out on the farm so you won't have to worry about money.'

Simon stopped going to school. Duardo apprised his peer farmers of the recent developments. It had already been two weeks since Simon had gone to school. He and Duardo led the farmers in plowing the fields, while Ka Tindeng prepared their lunches. They also managed to plant the crops.

In the third week, Simon went to school. He was more worried than ever. His grades started to drop and the principal warned him that he might not be able to graduate.

Henceforth, Simon started studying even more diligently. He attended school alongside working at the farm. Just before sunrise, he would be on his way to the fields to plant the crops. Wasting no time, he would change his clothes there and rush to attend his classes, early in the mornings. Later in the afternoon, he would come back to tend to his crops.

He was no longer courting Elena. His father's illness was another reason for him avoiding her. One day, however, he was surprised to see her talking to Alejandro Borja in school. They were both sitting on a stone bench under the shade of a tree. No one else was around.

That afternoon at school, he saw Elena studying alone at the library. He was about to leave when she stood up and called out to him.

'Please do not leave, Simon.'

Simon stood rooted to the spot. He did not know how to react.

'Are you avoiding me?'

He remained silent.

'I looked for you when you were absent. I asked around. They said you were at the fields. I thought you had dropped out of school.'

'I should stay away from you, Elena,' Simon replied. 'You are the daughter of our landlord. You own the land we till.'

Elena felt dejected. 'Please don't say that.'

'You shouldn't look for me. Andro is the right guy for you.' Elena stared at Simon's face and he grew more and more nervous. She gripped his arm.

'I looked for you, Simon, despite my father's warning.' She was crying now.

Simon ignored her and walked away. He missed Elena, too, but at this point, she should be the least of his concerns. His father was sick, and as Tano's only relative, it was Simon's duty to look after him.

Simon's crops had multiplied. The seeds were sprouting, and soon, the harvest season would be upon them. All the farmers could hardly wait.

Tano had recuperated enough to be able to step out. Even if it was against Simon's wishes, he still went to the carabao's pen at night and sharpened his bolo. One morning, while Simon was at school, Regente's steward passed by.

'The Spaniard has asked you to come,' the steward said.

'Why?' Tano asked in a tone of irritation.

'I don't know. I'm just following orders.'

'Will he take my harvest and leave nothing to me?'

Tano almost knew why Isauro Regente had summoned him. He had probably heard he was sick, and that Simon was tending to the farm. He got dressed and went downtown that afternoon. The Spaniard had just woken up when he arrived.

'Sit down, Tano,' Isauro Regente began. He was as old as Tano, but had only a few grey hair on his head.

Tano took a seat.

'I heard you are ill,' Regente continued, still standing. 'I don't wish to do this, but since you can no longer work, I will assign somebody else to take your place at the farm.'

'Simon, my son, can take my place,' Tano suggested. 'He is not ill. He is still strong.'

'Simon,' Regente remembered his daughter's suitor. Alejandro Borja had once told him that the farmer's son and Elena were starting to like each other.

'I will assign somebody else to work for me, Tano. I have already given my word.'

Tano could not say anything.

'He will take your place during the next harvest season.'

Tano's steps were heavy as he left Isauro Regente's house. The students had already been dismissed from school. Outside the Regentes' gate stood Elena.

'Good afternoon, Tano,' she greeted him.

Tano could hardly hear her. He kept walking. He was looking straight ahead of him, at the road. He coughed occasionally, but still kept up his pace. Regente was firing them. They would no longer be able to work at the farm.

'So what if he fires me?' Tano asked himself. 'It's no big deal.'

But what would become of them after they'd been let go? *How will we survive?* Tano's shoulders dropped. He was confused more than ever before—his legs were getting more restless and his knees were shaking. He did not know what to do. For more than forty years, he had been working at that farm; now, all of a sudden, he had lost it because he was ill.

'Was I not good enough, Regente?' he said aloud, walking alone. 'What did I do wrong?'

What did justice mean to Regente? Where was God's justice? For forty years, he had farmed the field; witnessed locust and raven infestations. Regente was utterly contemptible. Tano balled up his fists.

He did not walk along the path to their village. He did not want to go home yet. He wanted to go to the farm. It was already dark, but he still wanted to visit his farm. Along the way, he thought about his younger days; he saw himself as Simon—stocky and strong. And yet he also saw himself as a fading speck: a weary old man with drooping shoulders, coughing, withered, past his youth. Where was his justice?

He sat on the doorstep of their hut. He saw men selling smoked fish. As he looked up at the sky, he saw a cluster of stars. Lo, so many stars and so far away—just like his dreams of having a better life. He then remembered his carabao who needed to be fed tomorrow morning.

'I'm going home,' Tano said aloud. 'I can't just stay here.'

He was going home. The whole day, he had been attending to his carabao's pen. Simon finally came and told him to come home. 'Come inside, Father.'

'Go inside, son!' Tano chided his son. 'Can't you see I'm busy? Go on ahead and eat without me.'

Another day when Simon asked Tano to join him for supper and his father refused. That night, Tano wanted to tend to the carabao's pen and sharpen his bolo. He wanted to improve the pen and make his bolo as good as new.

The village was usually awake early in the morning. The peasants slept early at night. They were usually fast asleep by eight o'clock in the evening so they could wake up before sunrise. Their tired bodies found it easy to fall into deep slumber merely after heaving a long sigh that expelled the fatigue from every nook of their tired chest. They had big appetites—dried fish was enough for them to eat with their steamed rice, and in case there was carabao's milk, they would pour it on top of the rice as well. Then they would scoop up rice with their fingers and eat large bites. They would then drink lots of water, gulping it down their throats.

The farmers left their wives to take care of their children and look after their homes. At noon, when their infants would beg for milk, the housewives would drop whatever they were doing to expose their breasts and nurse the infants. With so many chores left to do, the mothers would put their infants to sleep with a lullaby:

'Flying butterflies at the farm,
They hurry upon reaching the middle of the
road . . .'

The delicate sun rays penetrated through the canopy of the mango and bamboo leaves; the play of the branches and leaves made the shadows on the ground dance in the wind; smoke rose from the leaves burning in the housewife's yard; the hens clucked their tongues and dug the ground in search of food; the rooster crowed while perching on the edge of a fence; the sparrow flew from one branch to another at the top of the camachile tree. The silence put the infants to sleep.

That night, the moon was glowing. The huts were bathed in bright light. It seemed as if a long white rag had been laid out on the road between them.

In the neighbourhood, the children were playing tag. They were shirtless; they had doubled the thickness of the markings on the road so they could see the squares easily in the dark. They would shout when an opponent was tagged, and giggle when their teammate managed to escape.

From the hut's window, across the dama de noche tree, a boy sat with his mother, staring at the moon. The mother taught her child a poem detailing a dialogue between a farmer and the distant moon:

'Moon, moon, drop me a knife.'
'What will you do with the knife?'
'Cut a bamboo branch.'
'What will you do with the bamboo branch?'
'Build a barn.'
'What will you do with a barn?'
'Store rice grains . . .'

The window beside Tano's bed was open. The cold moonlight kissed his face and chest. Simon moved to close the window, but Tano stopped him. 'You might get cold, Father,' Simon told him, but he insisted. That night, he wanted to feel the gentle breeze; he wanted to inhale the fragrance of flowers in the night; he wanted to see the full moon.

When Simon closed the window, night had fallen; he saw his father lying still with his eyes closed. He nervously touched him and felt his icy cold hand. He called out to him and when there was no reply, he embraced his father's emaciated chest and burst into tears. The children suddenly stopped playing on the streets; they rushed to open the gates and enter their huts; their footsteps running up and down the abandoned road. They rushed to tell everyone they met that Tano had passed away. Shortly, the peasants rushed to Tano's hut. The children abandoned the squares drawn on the ground and gave up on their game of tag.

Upon Simon's request, Tano's remains were buried beside Melang's. The farmers carried the casket, with Simon and Duardo leading the way. Behind them was Ka Tindeng and her daughter, Saling. Hulyan and Nazario were among those who shouldered the coffin; the peasants and their wives and children followed after.

The men at the end of the small procession were talking.

'Tano can rest now,' said one elderly farmer. 'That guy would never rest while he was still alive. May his soul finally find eternal repose.'

'Simon is an orphan now. Will he take the place of his father in the fields?'

'I heard the Spaniard rejected him.'

'Is that so?'

'What will become of his son now?'

There was a slight cool breeze as the funeral procession passed through the village and the leaves from a bamboo tree started to fall one by one onto Tano's coffin.

Simon tied a piece of black cloth around the right arm of his white polo shirt. He remained beside his father's coffin, the whole time. Duardo glanced at him occasionally and could see that he was trying to hold back tears.

Like Melang, Tano's grave was also laid beside the cemetery. There had been rumours going around that Paterno Borja was planning to buy this piece of land to convert into a sawmill.

It was around five o'clock in the evening when the funeral rites ended. The villagers started to go home. Duardo stayed behind with Simon, who was still looking at his parents' tomb under the acacia tree.

Since the start of the funeral rites, Duardo had been searching for someone. Could she have heard the news?

He was looking for Elena. But there was a chance that Elena might not have heard about the death of Simon's father. Duardo looked around the cemetery and was surprised to see a fair-skinned woman in a horse carriage. *Elena.* She seemed to be visiting the graves of their loved ones—as well as Simon's parents—looking at Simon from afar as she sat in her carriage.

'Simon,' Duardo whispered.

Simon lifted his head. The carriage Elena was in, sped away.

'She was here to offer her sympathies,' Duardo told him.

The carriage had already gone far, but Simon still stood looking at it from the periphery of the cemetery.

It was already January by the time Simon started reaping and milling the rice. He had been able to harvest two hundred and fourteen sacks of rice. He divided the sacks and gave Isauro Regente his share. His own share, in the meantime, was used to pay off their debts. They had incurred huge debts paying for Tano's medical treatment and funeral.

Simon was all alone in their house now. Both his parents had passed away. He was left to fend for himself, which was scary to him, especially since he had only just finished high school and still needed a mentor like Tano to learn farming.

'You can stay at our place,' offered Ka Tindeng.

'Sure, why not?' agreed Hulyan.

'I will not leave our hut.'

'So much like your father!' Ka Tindeng exclaimed.

February. The days were getting colder.

March. The season of hot weather had arrived. It was already summer. At school, they were preparing for the graduation ceremony. The honour rolls were announced and both Elena as well as Alejandro Borja had been included.

Simon did not want to attend the graduation ceremony. He did not attend the rehearsals either. Now that his parents were gone, it seemed as if his education no longer mattered to him. But Elena made him change his mind once she was assigned to take charge of the ceremony organization.

'I'm not going to join,' Simon replied when Elena asked him if he was attending.

'Why not?' Elena asked. 'Please attend. Do it for me.'

'Anything for you,' Simon smiled. Elena had somehow managed to convince Simon that graduation ceremonies were a once-in-a-lifetime event and if he felt ready in the future, he would never be able to turn back time and attend once the opportunity passed.

Elena wrote out promising predictions for the future of the graduating students. She predicted that Simon would become a brilliant lawyer someday and Alejandro Borja, a successful businessman. For her other classmates, she predicted that they would become teachers, doctors, and engineers. Elena had high hopes for her classmates and dreamt of becoming a teacher herself.

'You shouldn't have included my name in there,' Simon told her.

'Why not?' Elena felt a little hurt.

'It's not that I don't want to, but I will never be able to graduate from a college.'

'Who can tell?'

In the front row seats, Andro and Elena sat beside each other for the ceremony. Elena wore an all-white dress. She had a flower brooch pinned to it at the chest. During the choir, Elena looked at Simon as they sang a song about success, while also bidding farewell. Later that day, Simon felt challenged; as he finished high school, would there be another term?

Then it was time for Elena to deliver her speech. She was welcomed with a round of warm applause. Her voice sounded joyful, and at the same time, intensely sad. She spoke about dignity of labour and the dignity of peasants, which according to her, should be the interest of her batchmates once they became successful.

Except Duardo, Simon had no other close friends who were attending the graduation ceremony. However, he was surprised to see Ador in the audience.

'I'm glad I was able to make it,' Ador remarked. 'I just arrived.'

Isauro Regente passed them by, together with the Borjas. Simon overheard that there was going to be a party at Borjas' residence to celebrate Andro's graduation, and Elena was invited, too. She shook hands with her graduating classmates.

'Thank you,' was all Simon could say. Elena beamed. As always, she wore such a sweet smile and her palms were so soft when they touched his. However, Elena had to cut their conversation short when her father called her.

Duardo, Ador, and Simon went home together. As they were walking down the road leading to the village, Ador suddenly asked, 'Are you going to Manila, Simon?'

'I'm not sure. I would love to, but I'm broke and I've sold all the rice we had saved when Father passed away.'

His voice was dismal. The road seemed much longer than it actually was.

'Don't let anyone stop you, Simon,' Duardo encouraged. 'I have saved fifteen sacks of rice. I could sell them for you. You can expect me to never study again. But you are smart, Simon, much smarter than Andro. Ador will be going to college and you should, too. Our village's hopes rest on you.'

Simon did not say anything. For him, it seemed impossible to get to study in Manila, especially after he had seen Elena and Andro at their graduation.

'Once you're a college graduate,' continued Duardo, 'you can come back to the village. Or do you wish to live in Manila and never come back? The villagers are sure hoping we could have two graduates from Manila.'

Simon had not yet decided what he wanted to do with his life. The only choice he had to make right now was whether or not to ask Regente a second time to grant him a piece of his land, but he expected to have no luck there. He came home feeling dejected. His father had left him a carabao, but what good could it do? Farming was their main line of work. He would go hungry if he only depended on livestock.

Since it was a holiday, Andro went to the village with his two cousins. They were all carrying guns and going to hunt for game. Everyone knew that the old man Borja was a sharpshooter; he would toss a coin in the air and hit it bullseye with his pistol. He probably intended to pass on his arms' dexterity to his son, because Andro always accompanied him to hunting.

Simon approached another landlord for a plot of farmland to till, but with no success. He was increasingly feeling more unproductive and impatient. One day, he visited Ka Tindeng and told her he wanted to sell his carabao.

'I'm going to Manila, Ka Tindeng,' he told his surrogate mother. 'I will look for a job there. In case I get hired somewhere, I will be able to study.'

Ka Tindeng could not protest. She had big dreams for Simon. He had been able to finish high school, which was a good start. It was no longer appropriate for him to work at the farm.

Before Simon left, he sent a letter to Elena. He explained how exchanging letters was the only way they could converse. 'But your father might read this, Elena,' he included. Aside from telling her how much he missed her every day, Simon wrote about his earnest desire to succeed, not only to avoid disappointing his fellow villagers, but to be an eligible bachelor to court Elena as well. 'Once I finish college, no one would be interested in my origins,' he explained.

Elena replied to his letter. She said she would also pursue further education, 'since San Roque is in dire need of teachers. Right, Simon? I fervently hope you succeed. I will pray for you, Simon.' Elena was religious and a member of the Hijas de Maria, or the devotees of Virgin Mary.

Simon sold his carabao to gather pocket money for going to Manila. There he stayed with Ador. Whenever Ador had free time at work or at college, he would show Simon around the city. He also helped him look for a job, but they had no luck. Ador was able to put himself through school because he was working at the same time.

Meanwhile, Elena was staying at a dormitory while studying education at a prestigious university. When Simon was still looking for a job, he wrote to Elena saying that he would use his salary to pay his matriculation fees. They continued to exchange letters regularly. In one of his letters, Simon asked if he could visit her. Elena replied by asking what was stopping him. Simon was ecstatic.

That week, he put on his one and only fine pair of trousers. He finally arrived, after a long search, at the dormitory where Elena was staying. It was so different from the room he was renting. The dormitory was huge and spanning across two floors, both well-maintained. He entered the reception area, full of well-dressed men. For a while, he had thought he looked his best, but comparing himself to the men at the dormitory, he began to feel like he did not belong there.

'Is Elena Regente here?' Simon asked the receptionist. The receptionist sized him up from head to toe.

'She's here. May I have your name?'

'A friend from the province.' Simon told her.

The receptionist asked a staff member to tell Elena that she had a visitor. Simon stood waiting, thinking of how to break the ice between him and Elena when she arrived. He had not informed her that he was going to drop by, but he was certain she would be delighted to see him. He waited for the staff's cue, when he suddenly saw a suave young man opening the door. He recognized the guy, and Andro instantly recognized him, too.

'Simon, what are you doing here?'

Simon was speechless. In front of Andro, he felt like disappearing. Andro walked around, his hands inside his pocket, and upon reaching the receptionist's desk, asked, 'Is she ready?'

'She will be here in a minute.'

'Elena is my date tonight, Simon.'

Simon did not stay for much longer. He stepped out as if he had been driven away. He crossed the street and from afar, when he turned around, he saw Andro coming out of the building with Elena. He gave a long sigh and murmured to himself that Elena could never be his. She was too out of his league.

Instead of wallowing in self-pity, however, Simon decided to prioritize his career above anything else. Luckily, he was able to find a job at a big construction company. He showed dedication and was an exemplary employee. Their manager was so impressed with Simon's performance that he made him supervisor of the timber inventory.

All Saint's Day was fast approaching and Simon had prepared for it. He planned to visit home to light candles on his parents' tomb. He stayed at Ka Tindeng's home for the duration of the short stay. He had bought skirts for her and a new pair of shoes for Duardo. In the afternoon, Duardo offered to accompany Simon on his visit to his parents' graves.

'We'll clean their tomb in preparation for All Saint's Day,' Simon told Duardo. 'Once I've saved enough, I will come back to have their graves marked with cement slabs. I feel sorry for their graves in their present condition. They might have been hidden by the overgrowth of tall grasses.'

Carrying a shovel each, Simon and Duardo went to the cemetery. While walking, Simon narrated to his friend the account of his experiences in the city, while Duardo listened silently.

They reached the cemetery. Simon knew the way to his parents' graves all too well. They passed by some men who were either digging or painting tombs with white paint.

'Someday, I will be able to repaint my parents' graves as well,' Simon told Duardo as he turned his glance towards a big tomb. It was made of marble, embossed upon which were the names of the deceased in memoriam, by their children.

Although Simon saw many tombs, he could not find his parents' graves. The shattered fence surrounding their graves had been replaced by a new cemented fence. He and Duardo tried to locate the graves.

'We might be mistaken,' Duardo told Simon.

'This is the spot,' Simon said as he dropped his shovel. 'I could never be wrong. Their tombs have no inscriptions.'

Simon climbed over the new fence to get to the other side. Piles of chaff covered the tombs completely. The tombs had been laid on public property, which explained why it was left unsupervised. Simon was very sure his parents' tombs were beside the acacia tree.

'This is the spot, I'm sure of it,' Simon reassured Duardo. 'The acacia tree has been bulldozed and replaced with a fence.'

They once again climbed over the new fence, which reached their necks. They approached an old man cleaning a tomb.

'Old man,' called Simon, 'would you know where . . .' He did not know how to ask him, 'Did you see a tomb there?'

The old man took his hat off. 'N-one . . .' The old man stuttered and Simon realized that he was cleaning his wife's tomb.

'Who ordered to build this new wall?'

The old man tried to speak straight. 'I don't know, son. But a certain Borja has bought that lot. He plans to convert it into a sawmill. Why do you ask, son?'

*They covered my parents' graves.* Simon couldn't say that. He glanced at the new fence. Vines had started to creep up its length. Still holding a shovel, Simon climbed over the fence again and his foot landed on soft ground.

'Are you sure that's the spot?' Duardo asked again.

'Where else would they be, Duardo?'

'Why would they cover the tombs? Don't they know someone's remains are lying there?'

Simon did not answer. He was almost certain he could never be wrong about this, so he started digging. Dig. Dig. Dig. The hoe reached the bottom layer, but there were no remains to be found. He went from one area to another and start digging again. Duardo wanted to help but he could not move from where he was standing. Was this the spot where the remains of Simon's parents had been laid? Most probably, otherwise, Simon would not have bothered digging. His brother by breast milk was already perspiring, but they still did not stop searching for the graves. Simon had just dug deep in one area, when a gunshot was heard. He suddenly stopped digging. They saw an old but big man approaching them.

'Hey,' yelled the old man, 'what do you think you are doing?'

The old man was Paterno Borja. He was holding a rifle.

'Why are you digging at that spot?' he interrogated Simon.

'This is where my parents were buried.'

Borja pointed his rifle at him. 'There's no grave there. This is not a cemetery. Look,' his left hand pointed to the nearby cemetery, 'That's where you should go.'

'I'm very sure this was where they were buried,' continued Simon. He tried to stop himself while—holding the shovel with his hands—his feet wanted to march up to Borja. Borja's rifle was on his side but ready to fire.

'When we covered that spot, we did not see any tomb or whatever. What we found was grass. There was no grave nor tomb. I have already bought this piece of land. Didn't you see the fence and the private property signage?'

Simon tried to lift his shovel but Duardo stopped him. 'Enough, Simon, enough.' He turned towards Borja and said, 'We will stop digging.' He held the crying Simon and walked away slowly. 'We will stop digging.' To make sure Simon didn't fight back, Duardo took his shovel and held him by his arm and apologized to Borja.

'I was excited to come home,' Simon kept saying. 'I couldn't wait to come home.'

Duardo looked at Borja walking away. They were still continuing to cover their plot of land. Men wearing face masks were unloading husks from three more cargo trucks.

'They have no respect for the deceased, Duardo. They did not respect my deceased parents.'

It was already very dark when they arrived at the village. Ka Tindeng was driving the chickens into their cages. The mother hen was caught first, and the young chicks started to chirp in panic.

Ka Tindeng noticed the sadness on Simon's face, and later that night, in front of the stove fire, Simon broke the news.

'I knew their tombs would be displaced,' explained Hulyan, 'but they could have at least told you where they moved them to. Borja shows no compunction.'

It was then that Ka Tindeng remembered that rainy night on which Tano really needed to borrow Paterno Borja's car to take his wife to the hospital. 'He turned him down,' Ka Tindeng revealed.

Old wounds felt fresh again. Simon let out a loud sigh. He looked at Duardo, who was cowardly. If Duardo had not stopped him at the cemetery, he could have retaliated on behalf of his parents.

The next day, he went to look for the graves again. He had to; he just did not know why. He stayed there for hours. He stared at the cemented fence around Paterno Borja's property; he did not even try to go near it. Tears began to form in the corner of his eyes.

'Were you able find them, son?' asked the old man whom Simon had talked to the previous day.

Simon shook his head. People started arriving at the cemetery to clean the tombs of their loved ones. Tomorrow, the cemetery would be full of people offering prayers for their departed loved ones.

Simon did not linger at the cemetery for long. He left hurriedly. At the gate, he saw a horse carriage parked.

'Is there a vacant seat?' he asked the old coachman.

The man pointed at the vacant seat beside a grieving woman.

'I need a ride.'

Simon climbed into the horse carriage and it sped away at the height of noon. They travelled across the downtown streets. The horse never changed its pace. The coachman continued to whip it, too.

The coachman heaved loudly upon reaching the rural area.

'Wait for me,' Simon told the coachman upon reaching Ka Tindeng's hut. He jumped off. He grabbed his remaining pieces of clothing from the midwife's house and set off.

'Where are you going, Simon?' asked Ka Tindeng, who was shocked. Hulyan, Duardo, and Saling watched as the two talked.

'I'm leaving for Manila again, Ka Tindeng.' Simon embraced her. 'I will go back to Manila, Ka Tindeng. I will not return without a plan for vengeance. I swear, Ka Tindeng.'

Simon went out and got into the horse carriage. The coachman once again whipped the horse. Simon passed by his former hut, but did not look back. He met some farmers on his way, but he did not greet them. He held on tightly to the window of the carriage.

They reached the truck garage at the plaza. He saw
Paterno Borja's huge house. He deboarded from the horse
carriage. When a truck passed by, he hitched a ride. And
as they were travelling towards the city, slowly leaving San
Roque behind, his fury intensified.

The month of December rolled in. Christmas was near
and it could be felt in the air. Everyone looked forward to
the yuletide season. Aside from holiday vacations, it was
an opportune time for family gatherings and reunions, and
sharing a special feast to celebrate Christmas and New
Year's Eve.

Catholic devotees attended the Misa de Gallo, a nine-
day series of Mass, from 3–5 a.m., 16–24 December. It was
believed that one's prayers and wishes would be granted once
they completed the series of Mass. And of course, who else
would enjoy Christmas season the most but the children, who
were delighted to receive gifts and toys.

The harvest cycle continued. When the breeze combed
through the stalks of grains, they slowly bent their heads.
In the sky, the solitary fowl flew low; its wide wings spread
out. Sometimes, the scarecrow moved and squeaked; the
poor sparrows would not dare come near it. On top of the
mango and bamboo trees, kites would dance and bounce in
the air—children were flying their kites at the riverbanks.
Their skin had been burnt by the sun, as was their long
and rumpled hair; they giggled as they looked up in the sky.
The water from the river was shallow and clear; the wide
sidewalks were trodden by fishermen carrying their catch.
One fisherman had caught a new species of fish and he
suspected it to be a gourami—a weird-looking fish with

a beard—an omen of a major event. He had caught the fish from the same river one night, and said that a comet had suddenly fallen from the skies and almost struck him. He had been terrified.

The children in Ka Tindeng's yard got tired of flying their kites. They were playing rough games with their toy guns in the streets; they would hide behind the mango tree, behind the animal pen, underneath the basements. They carried wooden guns and swords. One of the children was Duardo's youngest brother, Imon. Imon was the most rowdy of the lot. He aimed his gun at a bigger boy and pretended to shoot, and when he refused to play dead, Imon screamed, 'You're dead, you're dead!' The bigger boy then challenged him back.

'Bang!'

'You're cheating! You're supposed to be dead!' Imon pushed the big boy; their other playmates started to laugh. As they gathered around both of them, some boys took Imon's side, while others thought he should play dead after the bigger boy had shot him. Saling, Ka Tindeng's only daughter, was at the window. She was beautiful. She braided her long, black hair; her clothes were too small for her now since she was growing up. Her nipples had started showing through around her breasts. 'Cut that out! I can't sleep with all that noise.'

'You're a grown-up, Saling, only kids nap!'

The kids did not stop playing. Saling complained to Ka Tindeng.

'Enough!' Ka Tindeng shouted. 'Hey, Imon,' she called to her son, 'come inside. While the rest of you,' referring to Imon's playmates, 'go home.' Ka Tindeng brushed away the wisps of grey hair on her forehead, 'You're all so noisy!'

Japanese Occupation of the Philippines began between 1942–45, after a war between the Japanese and American forces.

It was Ka Tindeng who first heard the news of an impending war; Hulyan learned that the American army was recruiting new soldiers and training them; that in Manila, people were practising drills and building air-raid shelters. 'We are fortunate that we're here,' Hulyan told his wife, 'in case of an air raid, we can easily seek refuge in the mountains.'

There was also news in the village about such preparations, but they had not formally been informed by the authorities. Local news was usually spread by word of mouth. Everyone was too busy to pay any real attention to what was going on, but they were aware of an impending war.

The devotee maidens of the Hijas de Maria (Blessed Virgin) were making preparations for the procession of the Immaculate Conception to offer prayers for peace. They adorned the church and agreed that all members would wear white and would attend Communion together.

And just as everyone had feared, the dreaded war broke out. The Japanese bombed the Pearl Harbor on 7 December 1941. All advance preparations lost relevance. From Manila, thousands of citizens fled to the province, pushing their carts, riding unconfiscated trucks packed like sardines; like they were seeking shelter from a volcanic eruption. Kids were crying, their parents were tired, but they continued to flee from the city. Behind them, smoke rose from the burning buildings.

The villagers started to evacuate, too. The farmers rode their carabaos, pulling wagons loaded with their belongings. One elderly man refused to leave with his children and grandchildren, saying he wished to die on his own land. Left behind with him were his hens, chickens, and pigs.

In the middle of a farm, a mother was clutching her one-year-old baby. Her hair was in a bun, her breast was exposed and clothes worn-out, and barefooted. She stumbled, but got up again, still holding her baby. The mother murmured a prayer, asking the Lord to protect her husband who had joined the army. Not very far, she could see her seven other children.

The city and rural folk worked together at the farm. Rich and poor treated each other like brothers and sisters. Those who begged for food were fed; the farmers were assisted by their carabaos in plowing the fields; together, they helped one another ensure a bountiful harvest to feed everyone. A farmer slaughtered a pig to be cooked and shared with the refugees.

There was a little boy only about a year old, who would always remember what he was witnessing. During the war, his family had sought refuge in an abandoned house. The boy heard a series of gunshots in the distance and squirmed against his mother's chest to feel safe as she firmly held him while saying a prayer.

Duardo had been working at the farm for two days when the men from Mt Arayat arrived. They were armed with guns and they promised freedom. In the fields, they seized the opportunity to open attack now that the war had broken out, to cause widespread chaos, influence and recruit more and more young men to fight for their ideals. They had the same oratory talents as the man Tano had heard at the plaza.

That night, they collected all the hay that had been left behind and made a bonfire. The chief of the rebels, whom they called Labaw, spoke. The full moon above served as the only source of light. The air was cold and they were wearing thick clothes. The farmers who were wearing long-sleeved shirts were his primary audience.

'Comrades,' Labaw began, 'the time has come. Let us all unite to defeat the Japanese; we will overthrow the government and start a new one. Let us fight for our freedom! In union, there is strength. We will fight for freedom, justice, and equality. From now on, there will be no slaves nor masters. We can finally be the owners of the land we till. We will free the next generation from slavery. We will all soon be free, brothers and sisters, if you come and join us!'

The peasant farmers listened attentively. They could not say anything because they could not articulate their sentiments as well. They just listened carefully to Labaw's promise of redemption. Equality for all: no master, no slave. Every man would own land; no division of social classes.

Ador, who had just come home from Manila, informed Duardo that their comrades from Arayat, over twenty thousand in number, all from Luzon, had been denied weapons by Quezon and MacArthur, even though their enemy was the same—the Japanese.

The Japanese appointed Paterno Borja as the president of San Roque. Borja was not in favour of his appointment, but the Japanese had to choose a man whom the townspeople of San Roque obeyed and respected. Everyone knew Borja was rich, famous, and powerful.

Unfortunately, peace was not restored. The brown race could never bow down before the Japanese sentries. They had sacrificed so much in the past four hundred years. The new freedom they were promised was not genuine either; there was no prosperity to be found in the Greater East Asia region, of that they were certain.

Furthermore, not a day passed when the Japanese did not arrest an insurgent and torture them using their armour and samurai at Captain Martin's house, which they had converted into a prison. The dark history of the mansion thus continued.

The Japanese became fiercer when their troops retreated and took a hiatus. The American rescue army was on its way; General MacArthur had kept his promise of 'I will return'. Using submarine troops, they distributed weapons and artillery among soldiers. The boxes they carried were loaded with rifles.

'The life of a guerilla is fraught with danger,
They march in the morning and become soldiers by night,
It is almost impossible to make a woman fall in love with us.
Say it aloud, Neneng—we climb mountains,
We sleep on fallen leaves and branches,
We cover ourselves with worn-out blankets,
During mealtimes, we eat sweet potatoes.'

The soldiers' theme song did not describe their actual experiences but it entertained them at night, when they camped in the mountains or the plains. The song also did not tell the story of the mother with a son in Bataan; the story of an elderly father of a guerrilla son, who went to a village and was killed there; the story of starving children, waiting for their father who was never to return; the story of a guerrilla who was ambushed, and even till his last breath, could never witness the freedom they were fighting for.

Isauro Regente was arrested by the Japanese for supplying rice to the rebel guerrillas. He was handcuffed and taken to

Captain Martin's house, but Paterno Borja defended him and refuted the allegations against him, and through his persuasive words, convinced them to release Regente.

A barber in the village had the opportunity to cut Labaw's hair, the one with the gift of gab; three days later, the barber learned that Labaw was among the casualties of the endless war between the insurgent's army and the Japanese guerrillas. Labaw had been beheaded and his body had been wrapped in a native mat and propped onto a hut's ladder. His body was later thrown into the river, but the one who had decapitated Labaw, paraded his head through the streets.

The corpses of the Japanese and Filipino drifted together in the river. A fisherman mistook a floating sack to contain coconuts. He grabbed it and out came strands of hair—the Japanese had killed all the prisoners they had held captive at Captain Martin's house.

The wrath of the villagers grew without bounds. Three Japanese soldiers arrested Diegong Laki, a rebel leader, and his three cousins, and took them to the deep blue ocean. There, they held their heads under water until they drowned.

The next day, two Japanese men arrived in the village. The townsfolk surrounded the two men and grabbed their arms. From the circle, a shot was heard, and one of the Japanese men fell to the ground. The remaining soldier was unarmed, and yet he resisted them. An elderly man suddenly ran into the circle pointing his bolo at the Japanese man. 'They killed my son; they killed my son!' cried the weeping old man. It turned out that he was Diegong Laki's father.

World War II ended on 2 September 1945. Sergio Osmeña was the incumbent Philippine president at the time. Finally, liberation had come. After the intense bombing, the coast had been ruined but along the trail of destruction lay the path to liberation.

Above the clouds over the village, an airplane was seen flying and dropping a star-spangled banner—a little boy was able to grab it, and started running down the streets, rejoicing. The villagers came out of their houses and learned that the Americans had arrived. General McArthur had made his proclamation (abridged).

> 'I'm back. With the help of our Lord Almighty, our armies have once again landed in the Philippines—a land blazing with the blood of our two races. We are here, ready to destroy the remaining traces of the enemy, and to restore, with unbreakable strength, the liberty of your people. The moment of your redemption has come. Let the memories of Bataan and Corregidor be our guide. Get ready as we approach the battlefields. Attack at every opportunity. For the sake of your loved ones, fight! On behalf of the heroes who put their lives at stake, continue the battle! Redeem the land that was once lost. Do not surrender your arms of steel. The Divine Lord will lead the way. Be steady in His Holy Name as you walk the divine path of Liberty!'

Peace was soon restored. The soldiers, the survivors of Bataan and Corregidor, returned home. They brought news of enduring torment. The guerrillas had descended from the mountains; the peasants carrying arms had returned to the village.

Each one had a different story to tell. It was long before they had finished talking about the chaos. Old memories were rekindled; the misfortune of a child had been accepted but not forgotten. A mother would always remember the last look on her son's face before he left for war; a child would always remember his father before he went into the battlefield.

In San Roque, they were waiting for Simon to return, but he never came. Could he be dead? Duardo asked those who had returned. They all had different guesses; some said they could not ascertain if it had been Simon whose body they saw; maybe it was just his doppelganger. Someone returned from the city and reported that Simon had been onboard the *S.S. Corregidor* that sank; or the steamboat that was headed towards Visayas when it crashed into a minefield of the Americans. The boat exploded and no one among the many passengers survived. Someone also told Duardo that Simon could have been killed in the Manila bombing.

Many returned, but not Simon.

# Part III

Return

1951

A decade had passed. Four Philippine presidents had succeeded Quezon: Jose P. Laurel (1943–1945), Sergio Osmeña (1944–1946), Manuel Roxas (1946–1948), and Elpidio Quirino (1948–1953). World War II had ended and the military was now controlled by civilian and democratic governments. Peace and order were finally restored.

So many things happen as each season passes: children go to school to receive their primary education, where they learn how to read and write; they start developing crushes in high school; some need to work at a young age to help out their parents; some move to Manila either to continue their studies or to look for better prospects; babies are born every minute, seeing the world for the very first time; people grow weary and tired until they bid their last goodbye . . .

In San Roque, the El Niño drought had taken a toll on the farmers' crops. The villagers could only hope it would rain. In an attempt to build channels to irrigate their crops from the river, a bulldozer was driven across the Pampanga, but it was too shallow.

The farmers went home broken-hearted. They had to return empty-handed from the farm. Nothing could save the wilted crops, which were now almost ready to be burned for fuel.

'How long will this drought last?' they lamented.

In an attempt to make the dry season go away, they resorted to desperate measures, putting their faith into religious statues and images. Tandang Flora brought out a statue that a swimmer had found at the bottom of the Pampanga River. Deeming its discovery to be miraculous, the villagers believed that worshipping the image could bring about rains. According to urban legend, the blessed statue was part of the debris from a ruined church, but then how come it bore no resemblance to any saint? Nonetheless, they had nothing to lose from resting their hopes on this statue. They held a procession to pay their tributes.

'Our Father, who art in heaven, hallowed be thy name.'

They prayed with their eyes closed as they moved the beads of the rosary, one by one.

'Give us this day our daily bread, and forgive us for our trespasses . . .'

The children and other worshippers inside the church were cued to answer with 'Amen, Jesus!' and cry aloud, 'Rain! Rain! Come, rain!'

Mariang Basahan also joined the procession. Until now, she had not borne a child—and she would never be able to any more, since she was way past the age and had stopped menstruating. Her husband once threw her out of their house, but she chose to stay and be a willing victim and his doormat. She just could not leave him because she had no other place to go, and old age was catching up to her. As always, she would wrap rags around her stomach, still hoping for a miracle.

The procession was held for days, but there was still no sign of rain. 'Pray harder!' Tandang Flora would yell at the children, who he thought were not sincere enough. The children stomped and shouted. 'Rain! Rain! Come, rain!' Their voices in unison could be heard from afar, but could not reach Heaven.

The villagers were contemplating whether they should still celebrate Thanksgiving Day. They were able to reach a consensus that they would, but without the lavishness of last year's celebrations. It was enough to hold a Mass after the *novena*, followed by a simple feast. Wearing their best clothes, the villagers went to church and offered their prayers, asking God not to forsake them, to bless them with food on their table, to keep them from getting sick, especially because heavy labour was part of their daily lives.

It did not take long for their prayers to be answered thereafter, or perhaps, it was pure coincidence. At last, the rains started pouring. How come the weather seemed unpredictable even to them at times? They would wonder. Some wise men from the village would say this was being brought about by the current trends of industrialization, leading to climate change.

There had been many changes in San Roque in the last decade. The village road connected to the national highway. It was once a mere trail and was now covered with asphalt, which made it easier for farmers to travel to their fields. There had been rumours going around that a wealthy man had been able to purchase a piece of land near the national highway. Who could he be? There were also rumours that someone had bought Captain Martin's big house. Why would anyone be interested in living in the Spaniard's house that was almost certainly haunted?

The rural and urban folks both wondered. They suspected that someone from the city had bought that piece of land; someone who belonged to the upper class, but that was hardly possible since land in the rural areas was not available to them to buy.

It was not too long before a few men arrived at the captain's house. They started renovating the mansion, then painted it all white. What used to be an old prison had now been sanitized and made immaculate by the white paint. The villagers learned from the construction workers that the house was going to be converted into an agriculture school.

The next thing the villagers noticed was that truckloads of construction materials were being brought to the site: gravel, sand, galvanized steel, cement, and timber. Who could this wealthy person be, who had chosen to build a huge house beside their poor huts? The construction materials were surrounded by fences bearing 'Do Not Enter' signs.

Soon, electrical posts were erected beside the mysterious building. Just beside the new building was built an equally mysterious mansion, which covered the entire premises of the captain's estate. The townsfolk assumed that the mansion and building belonged to the same owner, since they were in such close proximity.

Just when the mansion and the building were almost complete, two men arrived in a swanky black car. The one driving the car was younger than its middle-aged passenger. Who could they be?

The two men inspected the properties. Renovations were made using a combination of traditional and modern architectural elements. The building and mansion were surrounded by cemented fences and a steel gate, and had their own garage; the front and backyard were landscaped beautifully with ornamental plants, trees, and hedges.

'I will fill my garden with many trees,' the man with grey hair said. 'Now is the perfect time to be planting trees. Indeed, you are lucky if you have your own garden in this village; to have your own land and the liberty to do as you wish.'

'Most of the peasants can never have their own estates,' the younger man replied.

'You will like it here, Manuel.' Manuel nodded, 'I guess so.' The furniture inside the mansion was all brand new. Manuel sat down on a huge sofa. 'While coming here,' Manuel said, 'I was wondering why you invested in a school and not in another business.'

'I love this village, Manuel. I wish to help my townsfolk. I have mentioned before that I used to be a farmer, just like them.'

'Yes, I remember.'

'It's time to change their destiny.'

'You have high ideals.'

'One should start somewhere.'

'I agree. But we can never be too sure that many will register.'

'It's not important how many students we have.'

'Only a few farmers are willing to be taught. For many of them, first-hand experience of working in the fields is enough.'

'That's one of our challenges, Manuel. We believe that by using more innovative methods, we can increase farm yields. We have to teach them survival skills in farming.'

'That would take a lot of hard work.'

'It's worth a try.'

Simon was now a self-made man. He had been in Mindanao when the war had broken out. He was a lost soul, a seed looking for a breeding ground. He had come far from being a timber-inventory clerk. His employer had promoted him until he had gathered the means to start his own business. An insurgent killed his employer during the Japanese Occupation. After liberation, Simon succeeded his employer as the owner of the business and was granted a concession to use one of his properties. He became successful in his business and within a span of ten years, became the owner of a large sawmill factory. His main office was in Manila. With the help of his workers, he was able to expand his business to almost half of the Luzon archipelago, and now he was planning to start exporting his timber internationally. He had indeed come a long way from being a farmer to a business tycoon. He spoke little before and had become even more silent and reserved recently, focusing solely on his business.

Simon had met Manuel at Cagayan de Oro. He had been a student of agriculture. Simon had encouraged Manuel to come with him to San Roque. Manuel was still young, full of hope and very trainable, and he immediately accepted

Simon's invitation. Holding a degree from Los Baños, Manuel was no stranger to the farmers' condition in Luzon. Simon wanted to see how his hometown had changed, so he invited Manuel to tour the whole village with him. They passed by Isauro Regente's house. He remembered how his father used to drop by the Spaniard's house to give him his share of their crops. The Regente house was now in ruins. Then they reached the house of the Borjas. Simon looked in through an open window. No one was there. He turned to Manuel and shared his sad story with him, 'I almost cursed this town. That house belonged to a wealthy man named Paterno Borja. He refused to help my father take the woman, whom I never had the chance to embrace and call "Mother", to the hospital in his car, even when it was a matter of life and death. The Borjas dug out my parents' graves without my permission. The peasants are treated like slaves in this town, Manuel!'

They were able to tour the whole *población*. The town had become more populated with the passage of time. No one could recognize Simon. He decided to visit their old hut and remember his roots once again. *Would our hut still be standing?*

Their hut was still dusty; nothing had changed. Simon began to wonder how Ka Tindeng and Duardo were doing. He stopped his car and parked it near their dilapidated hut. He stepped out and found that their hut no longer stood there—the spot was entirely covered with tall grasses. He looked around. The camachile tree was still beside the carabao pen. He walked around, trying to recall the memories from his past, when he heard someone call out to him. He turned around and saw a man running towards him.

'Simon!'

Who could he be? The man seemed familiar. 'Ador!' The two friends embraced each other after a long time.

'I asked the children whose car was parked beside your ruined house. They had no idea, so I went to check it out. I knew it would be you. Long time, no see!'

'It has been a decade, Ador.'

'We were looking for you. We asked those who returned if they had seen you. How are you, Simon?'

'I should ask you the same, Ador.'

'I'm now a teacher.'

'I have come to stay here now,' said Simon. 'How is Ka Tindeng?'

Ador hung his head.

'Is she dead?'

She was dead. Dead. The woman who breastfed him had passed away. 'Duardo? Where is Duardo?'

Ador again remained silent for a while.

'Where is he?!'

'He was killed.'

'Killed?'

Ador nodded. Simon was shocked by the news. *Why would someone kill my brother?* Duardo and he were the same age. He was too young to die. He couldn't have died from an illness. 'How did it happen?' he asked again.

'Do you remember Saling?' Ador asked.

Simon wondered why he had suddenly mentioned Ka Tindeng's daughter. 'Yes, I remember her. Duardo's youngest sister.'

'Duardo loved his only sister dearly,' Ador said. 'What about Kabesang Bastian? Do you remember him?'

Simon nodded.

'Saling was only sixteen years old when Ka Tindeng sent her to Manila. Goodness! The poor child was crying when she learned she would have to work for Kabesang Bastian. I had started teaching by that time. Saling was a junior in high school when she left. "We can no longer afford your matriculation fees," Ka Tindeng had explained to her. "Hulyan and Duardo's income is not enough." Hulyan was growing old, Simon, and he had had to ask Duardo to take his place at the farm. For Ka Tindeng, it was enough for Saling, a woman, to know how to read and write. She would even compare herself to her daughter, saying how she was illiterate and she had done well for herself. I volunteered to pay Saling's matriculation fees, but there were other expenses to consider for the school.

'Kabesang Bastian (Chief Bastian) offered Duardo to send Saling to stay in his house. Duardo was obliged. He thought Saling was still young and could catch up at school. Besides, the chief might have terminated Duardo's employment too, if she refused. How else would they survive? We don't have much choice as farmers, Simon.

'So Saling served Kabesang Bastian as his house help. Poor Saling! She would often cry whenever she came home to Ka Tindeng. She had to volunteer to do all the chores around the house for as long as she had to live there. "Stop complaining, child," Ka Tindeng would chide her. "Your brother's job is at stake here. And like I always tell you, we can hardly make ends meet." Once Ka Tindeng's children were all grown-up, she was hoping the quality of their life would improve, but that dream shattered on the day Duardo died.

'One morning, Saling came home, shocked and speechless. "What's the matter, child?" Ka Tindeng asked her. That was when the poor child had a nervous breakdown, and Duardo feared his sister had been molested.

'Kabesang Bastian was his primary suspect. Everyone knew about his extramarital affairs and how he had several mistresses, loved going to nightclubs and flirting around with women. Saling was vulnerable, since she was a full-time helper at the house. It was very likely that she had been a victim, too.

'Duardo was so furious that he went straight to the chief's house. Allegedly, the accused offered to give him a piece of land in exchange for his silence. I thought Duardo would have accepted the offer, but I was mistaken. One night, Duardo broke into the chief's house. He poured gasoline on the sleeping man and set him on fire. The chief woke up and cried for help. His helpers heard him and called for more help.

'I have not seen Duardo ever since then. The attempted murder made him an outlaw. I feel sorry for Ka Tindeng. The cops threatened to take her to the police station if she didn't surrender her son. But Ka Tindeng had no clue where Duardo was hiding. If she could at least speak to her son, she would have encouraged him to surrender.

'During the time when Duardo was still missing, the mayor sent military troops to capture the rebels in our town. The troops knew rebels would try to avoid inviting suspicion, so they searched all the corners of the village. Unfortunately, they spotted Duardo passing through the cemetery instead. He was probably trying to visit Ka Tindeng.

'The troops were heavily armed. Duardo was outnumbered though he had guns. He lost his balance while running away from them and tried to exchange fires until he could no longer fight back, and fell onto a tomb. The gunshots were too many and his wounds were fatal; he died on the spot.

Andro was with the troops during the shooting, Simon, and we all know he is a sharpshooter like his father.

'We learned of this only on the next morning. We had heard gunshots that night, but we had been too scared to step out and find out what was going on. We were surprised to learn that Duardo was dead. His corpse was brought to the municipality. People swarmed the place to know what was going on. He was wrapped in a torn mat. Ka Tindeng, Saling, Imon, and I went too.'

Simon suddenly remembered the last time he had seen Duardo. He had thought of him as a coward because he had stopped him from attacking Paterno Borja.

'There was a bounty on Duardo's head,' continued Ador. 'I think they offered 5,000 pesos. According to intelligence reports, Duardo was one of insurgent's leaders headquartered at Mt Arayat. The soldiers fought among themselves over who killed him. It was the sergeant who was granted the reward, later on. Till now, the jeep that he had bought with the reward money is still running.

'We then brought Duardo's remains home. Only a few were able to attend his wake. Since then, Saling and her family decided to move on with their lives. They knew it was hopeless to fight for justice. They just continued working at the farm until Ka Tindeng passed away. Eventually, Saling lost her sanity and committed suicide, Simon.

'They shot Duardo like he was the most-wanted fugitive. He made the mistake of killing Kabesang Bastian. He could have sought legal advice, sure, but what difference would it have made? Justice can be bought. I feel so sorry for us peasants, Simon. We're always on the losing side. What will become of us? Someone has to take a stand.'

It was getting dark but Ador and Simon still had a lot of catching-up to do.

'I thought I would see Duardo when I returned,' sighed Simon. 'I am deeply saddened by the news. We were like brothers, breastfed by the same mother after my mother died.'

'The men from Mt Arayat descended from the mountains and tried to recruit the peasants,' continued Ador. 'Duardo probably thought of joining forces with them when Saling was molested. He sought protection from the insurgents, Simon.'

Simon could only shake his head. How many had suffered the same fate? Who was the real bandit? Who was the criminal?

'I remember what he said when you finished high school, Simon. He said you and I were the only hope for our village. He further said it was hopeless for him to continue studying.'

*He resorted to violence*, Simon thought, *but I will always remember him fondly.*

'Do you remember, Simon, what I told you while we were in Manila? That I wish to have a job in which I could be of service to our townsfolk?'

'Yes, I remember.'

'I got hired as a teacher after finishing college. I love our town, Simon. There were big opportunities available for me to work here and abroad, both, but I chose to stay here in our town. I will always remember what Duardo told us. I can never forget. Seasons change but the peasants' way of life never improves. We are both children of farmers, Simon. We can never deny our roots.'

If they were to turn their backs on the peasants of San Roque, who else would save them? Clearly something had to be done to change the course of their history.

'I built a school for the aged,' Ador continued. 'We only had a few enrollees at first, but then word spread like wildfire. It was a pleasure seeing the elderly approach and ask me to teach them how to read and write, Simon. I also established a farmers' association. I taught young men and women the proper way of caring for and breeding livestock. I did all of these things to help them.'

Simon continued to listen to Ador.

'The peasants encouraged me to run for Mayor. Perhaps they thought I have what it takes to be a leader. My wife and father were against it. But who else would speak on behalf of the peasants? I was pleased to have earned their trust. I did grant them their request. A mayor only earns half of my usual salary as a teacher. Was I after the prestige? You can never truly earn the people's respect if you abuse your position. My opponents had far more resources, Simon, the Borjas—do you remember them?'

'I can never forget.'

'The peasants supported my candidacy since the results of the elections were going to determine their fate. I supported fair sharing of land between farmers and landlords, and equal distribution of wealth. My victory would have signified the defeat of the interests of the wealthy, Simon, because I represented the peasants' voice.

'But they resorted to propaganda to destroy me. They told the people that I was their enemy. I did not expect they could brainwash our peasants, Simon! I'd taught so many of them how to read and write, but barely fifty people voted for me. I filed my candidacy for Mayor only to help our people but the Borjas bought their votes for five or ten pesos each. When will the peasants ever learn, Simon? They seem to forget they hold the key to their own freedom!

'Let me tell you the story of an elderly man. His name was Tata Selo. He was toiling away on his land for fifteen years. When he was about to retire, he did not give the landlord his share. Why should he, when he had already served him for fifteen years with his blood, sweat, and tears? Many of our farmers have the same story as Tata Selo. But how dare the old man keep the landowner's share! The landlord terminated Tata Selo's service, but the old man refused to leave. When he was insulted, he axed his landlord to death.

'The cops arrested Tata Selo. He was sent to prison. Many thought he had gone mad because he kept saying that his landlord had been unfair. He needed to save the crops for his retirement, when he would no longer be able to work. It was only fair that before he retired, he was allowed to keep the whole of his last harvest. The cops beat him black and blue. The Borjas—the feudal lords who claim to be public servants—never do anything to improve the peasants' lives, either.'

'I bought Captain Martin's house,' Simon told him. 'We will open an agriculture school there.'

'A school? You would only be frustrated like me then,' Ador warned him.

'Who will speak up for the poor then?' asked Simon. 'You lost the elections but do not forget your idealistic plans for the peasants. You said so yourself—that you will never forget your roots as the child of a peasant.'

Ador did not answer because he was still disappointed at losing the elections.

'Listen, Ador,' Simon tried to explain. 'We will build a new San Roque together. Leave your job and help me out. You can teach at my school. Together with Manuel, we can bring about change. In honour of Duardo's death and your loss in the elections, let us try once again. Your intentions are pure and for the good of our people. We are not after profits but the betterment of our town. Let us combine our strengths and resources to uplift the peasants.'

Ador was thinking of something else. He had the same plans as Simon.

'Have you seen Elena, Simon?' he asked.

Simon could not answer. He looked at Ador. 'Not yet.'

'She married Andro.'

'Andro?'

Simon lowered his head. Ador regretted breaking the news.

Simon knew communication was vital to every relationship, but he had had to make compromises. While he was in Surigao, Simon met a teacher. He thought she could help him forget about Elena. He was a lost soul and the teacher gave him a reason to live when he was drowning in sorrow; she comforted him. He almost thought the mere presence of a woman during those dark hours could fill the void. However, the memory of his beloved always lingered; the only woman he had ever loved seemed so far away, like a star in the dark night sky.

Simon could never forget his first love. During his youth, as a poor farmer, Simon had felt he did not deserve her. But now that she had married Andro, Elena was no longer attainable.

'When were they married?' asked Simon.

'After the liberation.'

Ador could see that Simon was hurt. He felt as if he had missed a shooting star while he was toiling away. He wished he could have seen the star shoot across the sky for himself.

'Their wedding was quite the talk of the town in San Roque,' Ador continued. 'It was the month of May and the whole church was adorned with jasmine garlands. Elena wore a very white wedding gown and looked like the Blessed Virgin herself. She was smiling when she got out of the car, but there was no sparkle in her eyes.

'The Hijas de Maria, whose member Elena had been, had made the preparations for the grand wedding. One of them sang "Ave Maria". Elena tried to control her tears. They then proceeded to the reception area. Their guests were from the upper class—the governor, the mayor, the privileged.'

'What about Isauro Regente?'

'He is dead. I learned that his dying wish was for his daughter to marry Andro.'

'Regente wanted to make sure that Elena marries someone who could ensure a bright future for her.'

'All fathers only want what is good for their child, Simon.'

'Andro was among those who killed Duardo. Is that good?'

'He is rich and therefore honourable. They have been married for a long time now, but they still have no children.'

*She can never bear Andro's child*, Simon thought, *because she does not love him.*

'But it was evident that Andro thought no other man deserved Elena more than him. He was marrying the most beautiful girl in San Roque. While Andro was dating her, he reportedly spoiled her silly with gifts to win her love, but you know Elena always had simple tastes. But she was treated like a doll and a trophy, Simon.'

Simon felt so dispirited. His heart broke into a million pieces. He wanted to hear more from Ador, but it was getting dark and they had to part ways.

'I will take you home.'

'Don't bother. My house is close by anyway, and I wish to walk.'

Simon had built a large sawmill in San Roque. Borja's workers had transferred to Simon's company because he offered much better wages. He and Ador opened the agriculture school together. Ador left his job as a teacher and on their soft opening, Andro and Elena were among those they had invited. The two did not come. Neither did Paterno Borja.

Manuel and Ador assisted the farmers with enrollment.

'I write slow,' lamented one young farmer. 'I will never be able to pass.'

'We will not only teach you how to write,' Manuel explained, 'but also how to improve the yields of your crops.'

'But we might not be able to afford your fees,' the young farmer hesitated.

'On the contrary, I must say our matriculation fees are very affordable,' Ador reassured. 'Your son can get the money from his share of crops. From ten sacks of rice, he earns about 100 pesos. That's how much the matriculation fees is. But rest assured, his education is a good investment that will pay back tenfold.'

The old man finally agreed. 'We will sell one of our carabaos,' he said. He turned to his son, 'And you. Don't waste our money. Study hard. I cannot leave you any inheritance.

Take this opportunity while I'm still strong and can work. If you don't study hard, you will end up like me.'

'Your son will receive hands-on training at the farm. His education will provide him with appropriate skills to increase his productivity.'

'Listen to their advice,' the man told his son.

The young farmer listened. Ten sacks of rice per year. He could produce that much every harvest season. The good news was that his agriculture diploma could further make him eligible to work as a supervisor in the farming industry.

'I will raise one pig for my son,' a mother told Ador and Simon. 'We can pay for his matriculation fees this semester. Next semester, we expect the pig will grow into an adult and then we can sell it.'

'Look,' another farmer nudged his son, 'you will soon go to school. Study hard, okay?'

The agriculture school became the topic of conversation among farmers and fishermen in the whole village. The new generation was no longer content following their parents' footsteps. They wished to change their fate as ignorant people; they were aware of the travails of working in the fields with the threat of typhoons looming, and from sunrise to sunset. They were about to change their destiny. They would no longer allow themselves to be enslaved by the feudal system. For a very long time, they had been toiling away on land that they could never own. It was high time that they got ownership of the land they tilled. For a very long time, the nation's progress was hardly noticeable. Promoting the interests of the poor was not in the interests of the oligarchs. Alongside technology and education, the government could promote better farming and fishing techniques and train the peasants to develop the appropriate skills to maximize their profits.

With the passage of time, Simon's agricultural school gained in popularity. Simon was sitting in his living room, one day, stroking his pet dog—as he did when he was a child—when Andong, his helper, came in to inform him that he had visitors. Simon asked him to allow the guests to come inside.

The men removed their slippers and native hats. They were dark-skinned and stocky.

'Sit down,' Simon told his guests.

Their nails were chipped and their feet were calloused.

'Kindly serve our guests drinks,' Simon told Andong. He then turned his attention to his guests. There were five of them. Simon asked two of them about their children who were going to his school, and they replied they were doing well. Their spokesperson, Santiago, then told him their reason for dropping by.

'I hope you don't mind if we get straight to the point,' Santiago began, 'in order to avoid wasting each other's time.'

'Let's hear it.'

'We came here to discuss Ador.'

'Ador?'

'We've been trying to convince him,' continued Santiago. 'We wish to nominate him for the upcoming elections.'

Simon smiled. He was aware that the peasants were jaded with politics, so he did not quite expect that they would be interested in the elections at all.

'But Ador lost the previous elections, right?' Simon asked.

'Yeah, but we wish to nominate him again this time, because he is like one of us but smarter. We have no other candidate in mind who is as qualified,' Santiago explained.

'What did Ador say?'

'He does not want to.'

'He was probably disappointed with the results of the past election.'

Santiago leaned towards Simon. 'We came to ask if you could help us encourage Ador. We have seen and heard about his plans for the poor, and he is the only one who can bring about change in San Roque. Definitely not Borja, who always has a hidden agenda and is only good at lip service. You think you could help us?'

Simon thought for a while.

'What do you think?' asked Santiago.

This was Simon's chance to complete his mission of vengeance. How could he ever forget the day when he had gone to the cemetery and found out his parents' remains had gone missing? When he had almost lost his mind digging through an entire plot to locate their graves and all of a sudden, the old Borja had fired his gun in the air to stop him? Now the Borja's sawmill was about to close shop; he somehow had to execute his plans of seeking revenge. He would torture the Borjas; he would purchase and destroy their remaining businesses. If he supported Ador's candidacy and he won the elections, the Borjas would fully recognize that his power, influence, and money were far greater than theirs.

'I will help you.'

'What if we see Ador today?' Santiago suggested.

'Good idea,' Santiago's companion agreed.

Simon called for Andong and asked him to start the car's engine. Andong would drive them.

Ador's house was across from Ka Tindeng's hut. His house was as humble as a home could be. Its architecture and interiors were simple and comparable to the other peasants' huts. In fact, they still had a carabao's pen in their backyard, too. Ador had repeatedly asked his father, Nazario, to stop working, but the old man wouldn't listen.

The farmers took off their hats before entering Ador's house. His wife, Elisa, invited them in. Together with Simon, they all ascended the stairs to the doorstep. The farmers removed their slippers as they entered through the door.

'Good evening,' they greeted the old man, Nazario.

'Come in, come in,' Ador and Elisa tried to make their guests feel comfortable. 'I'm sorry if our house is too small,' Elisa said as she took their sleeping child from the bamboo bed into her arms.

'Please have a seat,' Ador said, smiling.

The guests sat on the bamboo chairs in the living room. Nazario offered them some coffee. Ador's diploma was hanging on the wall, which showed how proud Nazario was of his son. He considered his college degree a huge achievement, since he had failed to uplift himself as a peasant.

A lamp was lit and placed between Ador and Simon.

'What can I do for you?' Ador asked. He could almost guess the reason why they had dropped by, since Santiago was a frequent visitor.

'We requested him to come with us,' Santiago replied, gesturing towards Simon, 'to discuss our plans with you again.'

'You asked Simon to help you change my mind?'

'Yes, son!' exclaimed Santiago. 'And he agreed to help us.'

Ador turned to look at Simon.

'Why don't you try again?' Simon asked him.

One of Ador's four children approached him and clung to his leg. Elisa, too, joined them in the living room. She had changed her clothes to appear more presentable before Ador's guests.

'That's what we came here for, Ador,' said Santiago. 'Why don't you try again?'

'You asked Simon to come with you so I could not refuse?' Ador replied. 'I have had enough of this.' He turned to Simon. 'You can see that my family lives in a small house. In our present situation, how will I be able to compete with the Borjas? It's like a clay pot competing against a steel pot; a wagon against a car. Simon, we are nothing but ordinary folk of the working class. Elisa and I have dreams of building at least a more liveable house than this.'

Simon did not give up. He fixed his gaze on Ador.

'Are you scared, Ador?'

'It's not that I'm scared—I just have to look after the welfare of my family.'

'It was you who said that you wanted to hold a public office because you wished to serve the farmers,' Simon reminded him.

'Yeah. And I am serving them . . . as a teacher at your school.'

'You are indeed scared, Ador. I remember you saying you wanted to further your cause even more. We both want things to get better.'

'Will getting involved in politics make a difference, Simon?'

'Once you're a politician, you can actually implement changes.'

Elisa re-entered, holding a tray of cups filled with coffee. No one touched their cup.

'Entering politics is not simply a matter of nurturing idealism,' Elisa commented. 'We're fed up of it. I'm sorry to interrupt.'

'We all want change in San Roque, right, Ador?' Simon continued. 'Why don't you try again? It would be easier for us to actualize our dreams once you're holding a high position. Nothing can stand in our way then and we can finally defeat those rich and powerful people at their own game.'

Ador contemplated for a while. *I will prove to you, Simon, that I am not a coward. This is my chance to prove that I am willing to fight for my ideals.* 'Fine, I agree.'

Santiago stood up. 'Ador has finally agreed,' he told his fellow farmers. They all stood up, about to congratulate Simon and Ador, while Elisa and Nazario stood and watched them in silence. Nothing could stop Ador now.

'Alright, alright, I agree, but only on one condition,' Ador told them.

'What would that be?'

'We will not spend money on the election. We should not follow Borja's strategy. Let the people decide for themselves. If we lose the elections, it only means this is not the right time to fight for our cause. If we win, then God is on our side. Let the people be the judge. Would you join me in my experiment, Simon?'

Simon could not answer. What were their chances of winning in the elections if they didn't use money?

'I know what you're thinking,' Ador guessed, 'and maybe it's you who is scared. You are scared, Simon, not me. Where is your confidence, Simon? Where is the peasant's blood in you?' He probed further, 'Well?'

'Deal,' Simon said.

Thus Simon and Ador began working on their dreams. 'The peasants are on our side,' Ador would tell Simon. 'Putting their faith in an honest election will change their situation.'

Simon and Ador were both burning with passion to fulfil their dreams of uplifting San Roque, alongside Simon's own agenda to seek vengeance. More and more people were drawn to their campaign. 'Let the Borjas spend their money. Let the voters decide their leader,' Ador declared with confidence.

They went to the población, where they knew they might not be able to count on the people to be on their side. The oligarchs who were loyal to the Borjas lived in that neighbourhood. Andro was under pressure because his business had taken a turn for the worse with their sawmill closing down, but the Borjas were still willing to stake everything they had to win this fight. Borja called for his supporters and gave them specific instructions to deflect Simon's plans. He reassured his friends and business partners that they had very good chances of winning the elections. On the other hand, the peasants supported Simon and Ador's campaign in the hope for a brighter future for San Roque.

One evening, after a day of condemning Andro's political party in strong terms, Simon had an unexpected guest.

'Who is it?' he asked Andong.

'A lady.'

'What does she want?'

'She wants to speak to you.'

'She does?' Who was this lady? Simon stood up and Andong escorted him. When Simon opened the door, he saw the woman standing near the steel gate. It was Elena.

Elena was wearing a simple dress, standing alone by the opened gate. No one else was with her on that night and she appeared almost like an apparition to Simon.

'Good evening,' greeted Elena as Simon approached her.

'Elena,' Simon called.

Her hair was tied in a bun, but she still looked haggard, with dark circles around her eyes. Her soft, white fingers were holding the gate. By the looks of it, she seemed to be hesitating to come inside to meet Simon. But it was too late to back out now. He was already standing in front of her.

He stared at her face in surprise. The once-blurry face from his memories was now in front of him. He remembered how on countless nights he had struggled to put the pieces of the image together, but it was slowly fading from his mind. Earlier, Elena's face was only in fragments of memory; every time he saw a woman with the eyes like hers, he would remember her; the same would happen every time he saw a woman with the same slender figure as her, too. He saw her in every other women's features, in small fragments, and he never thought of another woman.

'Come in, Elena.'

Saying her name was like music to Simon's ears, and now here she was—actually standing in front of him. Elena slowly entered the living room. Simon caught a whiff of her fragrant hair as she passed him by.

'Please, sit down,' Simon gestured towards the big sofa. Elena sat down. Now that she was inside Simon's house, she finally had to gather the courage to speak up.

'I would like to ask you for a favour, Simon,' she said.

'A favour?' Simon was a bit surprised. 'What is it, Elena? What do you want me to do?'

'You have done so much to destroy Andro already,' Elena was sitting upright now. 'What more do you want?'

Simon smiled. 'Why do you sound as if I was seeking revenge against him? Why would I?'

Elena frowned. Simon noticed the tiny wrinkles around her eyes.

'You destroyed Andro's sawmill by competing with him. Now he's bankrupt.'

'That's just part of the business.'

'Even now, you continue to ravage him.'

Simon laughed as he stood up. He took pleasure in seeing his enemy trade places with him. And right here, right now, the only woman Simon had ever loved—who Andro stole from him—was in front of him: begging and pleading for him.

'Simon,' Elena called, 'can't you forgive and forget?' Elena did not wish to beg, but she seemed desperate.

'There are things that are hard to forget,' Simon replied calmly but with bitterness in his voice. 'There are things that I can never forget, Elena. Where are the remains of my parents? Borja buried them under his sawmill. Who was the reason my mother died? Borja refused to help my father take her to the hospital, despite his earnest pleas. Who shot my brother, my friend? Elena, it was Andro—he was one of the men who shot Duardo several times until he fell lifeless on the ground.'

Elena had come to ask Simon for a favour, but she also wanted to make him feel guilty.

'Speaking of things I can never forget,' Simon recalled further, 'how can I forget the day I paid you a visit, and Andro was there, and he told me you were going out on a date with him? I felt like an unwelcome guest. I just watched you two, Elena. You have no idea how much it hurt. Why did you choose Andro, Elena?'

Elena lowered her head.

'Is it because Andro was a rich man while I was merely a farmer?'

'Enough, Simon. I'm leaving.' Elena poised to stand up. While her head was bent, she could see Simon's shoes in front of her.

'Don't go yet, Elena. I've waited so long for this moment. Did Andro ask you to beg me to spare him, something which he cannot do himself?'

'No one asked me to come here, Simon. Andro has nothing to do with it.'

Simon laughed. 'Why are you so defensive?' He still remembered the description of the day Elena married Andro. The whole church had been adorned with jasmine flowers to celebrate one of the grandest weddings in San Roque.

His guest turned away to avoid his stare.

'My father forced me.'

'He did? And you obeyed him.'

Elena was crying now.

'The rebels threatened to kill my father, Simon, and Andro's father intercepted them. I had to obey him because I feared for his life. I am weak, Simon, I'm . . .'

'You do not love Andro, Elena.' Simon's voice became gentle. 'I just know it.'

*It is me you love, Elena. You married Andro but you could never love him.* Simon could feel his resentment towards Elena subsiding. His dream of marrying her had been shattered, but she would always remain in his memory. He had heard it straight from Elena that she had been forced to marry Andro. And now she seemed completely defeated.

Elena stood up. 'I should leave.'

Simon watched Elena leave the premises of his house. She was hurrying past. The bright lights of the passing cars temporarily shone light on her figure, which turned darker as she moved away. *I'm alone and so are you, Elena.*

Simon was still standing beside the gate when he heard someone approaching. He turned around. It was Andong. He too had seen Elena leaving in a hurry.

'Who was that, Simon?' he asked.

'A . . .' Simon could no longer see Elena. 'An old acquaintance who just wanted to pay me a visit.'

*A memory. Elena would always remain a memory.*

The conversation had made Simon's heart feel heavier. At last, Elena knew his position. The Borjas also knew he was a different man now. Why was he still bent on destroying them?

'He left,' Andong told Santiago and his friends when they arrived and asked to see Simon.

'When will he be back?'

'He did not say.'

The men were disheartened. Ador was apprehensive that Simon may have withdrawn his support of their plans, but it was too late for them to withdraw from the election. They had already started with their experiment; the peasants had started expressing their support for Ador. Simon could not withdraw at such a time. Borja was unstoppable; and the people were counting on Ador. He could not retract his name anymore. There was no certainty of his victory, but he did not want to disappoint those who stood in support of his candidacy.

Simon suddenly appeared out of nowhere. He could never abandon Ador. He had made a promise—they needed to destroy the old system to welcome the new. He shared the same vision of a new San Roque as Ador. More than seeking vengeance against the Borjas, he was interested in helping the peasants. He and Ador would continue with their experiment. At the back of their mind, they were willing to stake their life and limb for the farmers at all costs.

'If at dawn you would need to leave a mark:
Here is my blood and spill it now, as you wish.'

Tonight, in the plains between Arayat and Sierra Madre, the distant, big stars seemed to light up the sky. How far were these stars? If you look up for one second, they seemed very near; but if you looked closely, they seemed to move farther away. The stars shone bright as if they were close, and yet were so far away.

There were only a few vehicles on the national highway. In the village, the farmers' torches were lighting their way. Tonight, they were going downtown to demonstrate their unity as farmers with one voice. Farmers from other villages were also going to gather here—they arrived in horse carriages, carts, and on foot. They were all right behind Ador and Simon. They would walk through the whole village; they would pass by the walls built by their forefathers through forced labour; they would pass by the Spanish general's quarters, and then they would proceed to the plaza.

*The Borjas were very bothered when they learned that the peasants were gathering at the plaza, that night. They had heard the news about Simon's return.*

Simon and Ador would occasionally check on the arrangements for their campaign to see that it was going according to plan. They had gained many supporters;

everything had to be organized well. The peasants must know that they were fighting for their cause. Santiago and Manuel held torches high and proud. Nazario, Tandang Flora, Mariang Basahan were also present—almost all the peasants in the area attended their rally.

*To the Borjas, Simon was a big threat to their business and candidacy. They decided it was best they destroyed Simon before he destroyed them. Borja's supporters in the village informed him that the peasants had set off for the plaza.*

*'We have to disperse them,' instructed Andro.*

At the plaza, Ador was invited to give an introductory speech, followed by Simon. Both men spearheaded the procession superbly, holding torches of their own. Manuel and Santiago stood right behind them. Their numerous supporters had followed them there.

*The old Borja confined himself in his room. It was hopeless. His informant told him they were far outnumbered. Simon was the reason for their downfall; the man who had built the school.*

'I just remembered Duardo,' Ador said to Simon as they were walking on their way to the campaign. 'He would surely have joined us if he were still alive. He shared the same vision, Simon.'

Simon walked upright. The light of the torches shone through his grey hair. 'I just remembered something, too, Ador,' he said. 'I remember the marine I had met before I came back to the village.'

'A marine?'

'He was elderly and had long, grey hair. While I was onboard his ship, the impatient passengers were all pressuring him to recite a poem. You should have seen him, Ador. You should have heard him. During our entire journey across the sea, he kept reciting Jose Rizal's 'Last Farewell' in three languages—Tagalog, English, and Spanish. Are you familiar with that poem, Ador? Rizal wrote that poem while he was imprisoned at Fort Santiago. The Spaniards found him guilty of rebellion, sedition, and conspiracy. It was his very last work, before he faced a firing squad at Luneta in Manila.'

*Andro was cleaning his rifle when Elena entered their room. A glass of beer was sitting on top of his side table. Andro had turned into a drunkard since the day his sawmill had gone bankrupt.*

'The elderly man was like a sage,' Simon continued. 'On and on he went, reciting the poem in three languages . . .'

*'You went there, Elena,' Andro grilled her. 'You cannot deny it.'*

*Elena was gazing at the stage in the plaza from their window. The light from the stage shone on her face. The old Borja remained in his room. Andro was getting anxious. He looked at Elena.*

The crowd had reached Simon's agriculture school by now. The flames from their torches shone on the white paint of Captain Martin's old house.

'Someday, Ador,' Simon said, 'the government will support our school. There will soon be change in San Roque. We are all counting on you, Ador.'

The peasants were now at the centre of the población. They had multiplied in numbers; some urban folks had also joined them. Now the plaza was full of people. The crowd reached the former general's quarters. They were moving in an organized fashion. The constabulary and police force surrounded the plaza to ensure a peaceful campaign. The crowd gave a warm round of applause to those climbing onto the stage. Ador got on first, followed by Simon. Manuel was the emcee for the evening. The crowd cheered when it was Ador's turn to speak.

'They're here,' Elena told Andro, 'There is no way you can stop them now.'

Elena had also turned against him! Andro once again gulped down his beer. Nothing could stop them now.

It was Simon's turn to give his speech. He spoke in a mild-mannered way. Never in his life had he seen so many people gathered in one place.

Andro went towards Elena and grabbed her arm tightly. Elena lost her balance and fell to the floor.

'Stay there, Elena!' he warned her. He then grabbed the rifle he was cleaning earlier.

'What are you going to do, Andro?' Elena felt faint.

'Wait and see.' He started aiming his rifle, ready to pull the trigger. 'Andro! No!'

'I love San Roque,' Simon proclaimed. 'We must all unite to build a new San Roque!'

A gunshot was heard on the stage. The bullet went straight through Simon's chest, causing him to fall down.

Andro, Andro!

There were witnesses who had seen the shooter. The crowd panicked and sought refuge in a nearby building. The constables were on full alert. From the stage, Santiago pleaded for the crowd to remain calm.

'Calm down, calm down!' Santiago instructed, 'Please calm down!'

The supporters looked out of the windows of the huge building. Ador was holding Simon's lifeless body on the platform. 'They killed Simon, they killed Simon!' he wept, telling Manuel what had happened.

The constables managed to arrest Andro. The old Borja stepped out of his room. What had his son done?

*In the master bedroom, Elena was crying.*

The peasants carried Simon's body to his house in the village. His huge house and garden could not accommodate the many sympathizers; some had to stay at the side of the national highway all night. Once again, they lighted their torches. The peasants stayed on vigil all night; they would wait until the break of dawn.

In the coming days, the election was going to be the talk of town. Simon was gone and so was the peasant's only hope. The next generation would ask, 'Who was Simon?' And the older generation would say, 'Simon, my child, was a farmer who was able to change his destiny. He had high hopes for the peasants, but everything was lost when he died at the break of dawn. Now that he's gone, we must strive to prove that it was not in vain. He will continue to serve as our light in the darkness; an inspiration for many to chase their dreams.'